# GALAXY ZACK

## HELLO, NEBULON!
## JOURNEY TO JUNO
## THE PREHISTORIC PLANET
## MONSTERS IN SPACE!

By Ray O'Ryan
Illustrated by Colin Jack

LITTLE SIMON

New York   London   Toronto   Sydney   New Delhi

LITTLE SIMON
An imprint of Simon & Schuster Children's Publishing Division
1230 Avenue of the Americas, New York, New York 10020
This Little Simon bind-up edition March 2016
*Hello, Nebulon!*, *Journey to Juno*, *The Prehistoric Planet*, and *Monsters in Space!* copyright © 2013 by Simon & Schuster, Inc.
All rights reserved, including the right of reproduction in whole or in part in any form.
LITTLE SIMON is a registered trademark of Simon & Schuster, Inc., and associated colophon is a trademark of Simon & Schuster, Inc. For information about special discounts for bulk purchases, please contact Simon & Schuster Special Sales at 1-866-506-1949 or business@simonandschuster.com. The Simon & Schuster Speakers Bureau can bring authors to your live event. For more information or to book an event contact the Simon & Schuster Speakers Bureau at 1-866-248-3049 or visit our website at www.simonspeakers.com.
Manufactured in the United States of America 0216 FFG
1 2 3 4 5 6 7 8 9 10
Library of Congress Control Number 2015959778
ISBN 978-1-4814-7599-0
ISBN 978-1-4424-5388-3 (*Hello, Nebulon!* eBook)
ISBN 978-1-4424-5392-0 (*Journey to Juno* eBook)
ISBN 978-1-4424-6717-0 (*The Prehistoric Planet* eBook)
ISBN 978-1-4424-6722-4 (*Monsters in Space!* eBook)
These titles were previously published individually in hardcover and paperback by Little Simon.

# CONTENTS

# GALAXY ZACK

## HELLO, NEBULON!

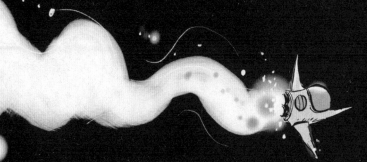

# CONTENTS

"Ooh! Look, Zack," called Shelly
Nelson from the front seat of the
Nelson family's space cruiser. She
pointed out of the large, round
windshield in front of her. "It's Venus!
And there's Mars!"

Sitting in the backseat of the

cruiser, eight-year-old Zack Nelson sighed. He knew his mom was just trying to cheer him up. But at the moment all he wanted to do was go home—to his real home, Earth. Not his new home on some planet called Nebulon.

Zack punched a code into the keypad below his window. The glass in the

window changed from dark to clear.

Billions of stars glittered in the inky blackness beyond the window. This was the part of space travel Zack liked best. Sure, he could see tons of stars with his überzoom galactic telescope back on Earth. But being out among the stars and planets, seeing them close up, always made Zack happy.

Except today, February 11, 2120. Moving day.

Glancing out his window, Zack looked past Venus and Mars. He had visited both planets many times. His family had often taken weekend trips to the Low Gravity Amusement Park on Venus. And they had always gone to the beaches at the Red Planet Resort on Mars for spring break.

But today all Zack could see was Earth. The tiny blue and white ball grew smaller and smaller in the window. The Nelsons' space cruiser zoomed farther away from the only home Zack had ever known.

Zack's dad, Otto, was up front in the pilot's seat, steering the cruiser.

"How ya doing back there, Captain?" he called.

Zack smiled. He was years away from getting his pilot's license, but his dad always called him "Captain" whenever the family took a space trip.

"I guess I'm okay," mumbled Zack.

"He's just sad because . . . ," began Charlotte.

". . . he's going to miss Bert . . . ," Cathy continued.

". . . and Luna," they said together.

Charlotte and Cathy Nelson were Zack's eleven-year-old identical twin sisters. They often spoke as if they were one person. They sat side by side in the seats next to Zack, finishing each other's sentences.

Zack's sisters had round faces with freckles. They both had flaming red hair like their father. Charlotte kept her hair in a ponytail. Cathy wore her hair in two braided pigtails. That was the only way most people could tell them apart.

"You'll still be able to talk to Bert, honey," Zack's mom said. Bert was Zack's best friend on Earth. "Between video chats and z-mail, it'll almost be like you never left."

"And Bert will take good care . . ."

". . . of Luna," said Charlotte and Cathy.

"You know that Bert . . ."

". . . loves dogs . . ."

17

". . . especially Luna," they added.

"The girls are right, Captain," said Dad. "Luna will join us as soon as we get settled on Nebulon. Then the whole family will be together again."

Zack just shrugged and stared out the window, watching Earth grow tinier by the second.

## Chapter 2
# Buggy Pizza!

"You'll love it on Nebulon, Captain,"
Dad said. "Wait'll you see the gadgets
they have there. They're way ahead of
Earth!"

"That sounds pretty cool," Zack
said. Then he grew quiet. *Dad's got
his great new job at Nebulonics, Zack*

thought. *Mom wants to start her own business. And the twins always have each other. They don't have to worry about making new friends.*

Zack leaned back in his seat and closed his eyes.

"Okay, class, time for our Zerbanese language lesson," said someone with a strange, high-pitched voice.

Zack's eyes popped open. He was in a classroom on Nebulon. All his classmates looked like monsters. And slimy creatures with dripping tentacles

sat all around him. The teacher looked like a giant two-headed snake.

Zack dashed from the classroom and ran across the street. He hurried toward a huge sign that flashed the words: THIS GALAXY'S BEST PIZZA.

Zack loved pizza. "Ah, pizza," he said. It was his favorite food. "At least they have *something* that

I know on this wacky, crazy planet!"

Zack rushed into the pizza place and ordered a whole pie. "I'll have today's special pizza, please."

Soon a steaming pizza floated down.

"YAAA!" yelled Zack. The pizza was covered with slithering worms and crawling

insects. It was topped with extra-moldy cheese.

Zack ran as fast as he could from the pizza place. He pulled out his video-chat hyperphone. Then he quickly entered Bert's z-mail address.

"Gotta talk to Bert," Zack mumbled to himself. "Maybe he can help me."

The screen on the hyperphone blinked. Then a message popped up: ERROR . . . CANNOT CONNECT TO EARTH.

"No!" cried Zack as he shoved the hyperphone back into his pocket. "I'm trapped here! And I'll never see or talk to my friends again!"

Zack felt a hand on his shoulder. Then he heard a familiar voice.

"Zack? Zack? Are you okay?"

Zack's eyes sprang open. He was looking up at his mom. They were still in the space cruiser, on their way to Nebulon.

"Bad dream, honey?" asked Mom, smoothing back Zack's thick blond hair.

"I guess so," Zack replied, rubbing his eyes.

A green light below the cruiser's front window began blinking. "Arrival on Nebulon in five minutes," said the cruiser's talking computer.

"This is so exciting!" Mom said as she sat back down in her seat. "Don't worry, Zack. This is going to be a great adventure!"

"Arriving on Nebulon in one minute. Please prepare for landing," said the cruiser's robotic voice.

"This is it, gang!" announced Dad. He was hardly able to contain his excitement.

Zack checked his safety belt. Then

he pressed his face to the window. His eyes opened wide as the planet below got closer and closer. Through thin pink clouds, Zack saw purple patches of land and large orange oceans. *Nebulon looks nothing like Earth*, he thought.

# Chapter 3
# Landing . . .
# Landing . . .
# Landed!

The space cruiser drifted down. Soon a busy spaceport came into view.

"What are those other cruisers, Dad?" Zack asked. He stared down at what looked like tiny flying space-ships. They zoomed around in the air.

"Oh, those are Nebulon cars,"

explained Dad. "On Nebulon, cars
and trains glide through the air. No
more bumps or potholes!"

"Landing . . . landing . . . landing . . . ,"
the computer repeated.

A few seconds later the Nelson's
space cruiser touched down on
Nebulon.

When they stepped outside, an

odd-looking man greeted them. "Welcome to Nebulon, Otto Nelson and Otto Nelson's family," he said.

Zack stared at the man. He was slightly taller than Dad. His head was egg-shaped, and his arms were long and skinny. They dangled down to his knees.

"Hi, Fred! Thanks for meeting us,"

said Dad. "Everyone, this is Fred Stevens, my new boss at Nebulonics."

Fred lifted his hand with his palm facing out. Then he moved his hand in a small circle in front of his face.

Zack looked at his sisters. "What is this guy doing?" he whispered.

Dad made the same movement with his hand. "That's how Nebulites shake hands," Dad explained. "Fred, this is my wife, Shelly."

Mom raised her hand and made a circle. "How do you do?" she said with a giggle.

"How do I do what?" Fred asked, looking very puzzled.

"That's how Earthlings say 'hello,'" Dad explained.

"Well then, how do you do?" asked
Fred.

"And these are my daughters,
Charlotte and Cathy," Dad continued.
"And my son, Zack."

"Nice to . . ."

". . . meet you . . ."

". . . Mr. Stevens," the twins said.

"Hi," Zack added.

"It is time to choose a car and go to your new home," said Fred. The Nelsons followed him into the space-port's main terminal.

They soon arrived at a big sign that simply read: CARS.

"We are here, Otto Nelson," said Fred. "I will leave you to choose a car. I will see you at the office tomorrow. Good-bye, Otto Nelson's family."

Fred Stevens left the spaceport.

Zack looked at the tall shelves under the CARS sign. Small boxes that came in hundreds of different colors floated in rows.

"Uh, Dad, I don't see any cars here," said Zack. "All I see are some box things."

"Welcome to Nebulon, Zack," Dad said. "Pick a color."

"Uh, okay . . . green, I guess," said Zack.

"Green it is," Dad said. He reached up and pulled a green box from the shelf. "Watch this."

Dad pressed a button on the box. It instantly changed into the coolest car Zack had ever seen.

"Hop in, everyone!" Dad said. "It's all ours."

"Does this thing have a GPS, Dad?" Zack asked as he got into the car.

"Better than GPS, buddy," replied Dad. "Look."

Dad pressed a button on the dash- board. "One twenty-two Zoid View,

Creston City," he said. Then he leaned back and placed his hands behind his head.

"Calculating," said a voice from the dashboard.

Without warning, the car sped out of the spaceport and into traffic.

# Chapter 4
# What a House!

The Nelsons' car flew through the air above Nebulon.

"One twenty-two Zoid View directly below," said the car. It slowed down as it approached a large house.

The house was shiny white. The car glided softly into a big, rounded

garage. It parked next to a smaller
red car.

"Destination reached," announced
the car. Then the engine shut off.

"Well, Nelsons, we're home!" Dad
announced. "Who wants a tour?"

"Me!" Charlotte shouted.

"And me!" Cathy agreed.

"Zack?" Dad asked.

"Uh . . . sure, I guess," Zack said, shrugging.

"Oh, I think you're really going to like this place, Zack," Dad said. "First stop—the kitchen."

Dad walked over to a round door in the garage. He went into a tiny room.

"*That's* the kitchen?" asked Zack.

"Nope. This is the elevator. Come on in, everyone."

The whole family stepped into the elevator. The door closed with a *whoosh*. The elevator took off—going sideways.

"The elevator connects all the sections of the house," explained Dad. "It travels through tubes. It goes up, down, forward, and backward."

The elevator glided to a stop, and the doors slid open.

Mom stepped into the huge kitchen. "Wow!" she said.

"Welcome home, Mr. Nelson," said a voice that seemed to be coming from every corner of the room.

"How ya doing, Ira?" Dad replied.

"Ira?" Mom asked. "Who's Ira?"

"Where's . . ."

". . . Ira?" asked the twins.

"*What's* Ira?" Zack asked.

"I-R-A is short for 'Indoor Robotic Assistant,'" Dad explained. "He's a computer, but he's so much more. Ira is part of the electrical, mechanical, computer, and communications

systems of every room in the house."

"Hi, Ira," said Zack, giggling a bit. *I'm talking to the house*, he thought.

"Welcome home, Master Zack," Ira replied.

*And the house is talking to me!*

"You don't have to call me 'Master Zack,'" said Zack. "Just 'Zack' is fine."

"Very well, Master Just Zack," Ira said.

The whole family chuckled.

"And welcome to you, too, Mrs. Nelson. Miss Charlotte. Miss Cathy."

"Ooh, I like . . ."

". . . being called . . ."

". . . 'miss'!" said the twins.

"So, who's thirsty after the long journey?" Dad asked.

"Can I have some orange juice?" asked Zack.

"Just plain old orange juice?" Dad smiled, and his eyes opened wide. "How about a jazzy Nebulon juice?"

"Sure, I guess," Zack said.

"Ira, can we please have a spudsy melonade?" said Dad.

"Certainly, Mr. Nelson," Ira said.

A small panel in the wall slid open.

Out popped a metal arm holding a glass of frosty, bubbling juice. "Here is your spudsy melonade, Master Just Zack," said Ira.

Zack looked at the glass with wide eyes. "Thanks, Ira," he said. Then Zack took it and gulped down the cool drink. "Sweet! Spudsy melonade rules!" *Maybe this place won't be so bad after all*, he thought.

# Chapter 5
## Wired!

"Why don't you kids check out your new bedrooms before dinner?" said Dad.

Zack and the twins stepped into the elevator. The door closed behind them and the elevator took off.

A moment later the elevator slowed

to a stop. The door slid open. Zack
stared into a large bedroom. It was
covered in pink. Frilly curtains hung
from the windows.

Zack shuddered. "Ugh! This is *your*

stop," he said to his sisters.

"Ooooh . . . ," said Cathy and Charlotte, running into the room.

The door zipped shut and the elevator sped off. A couple of seconds later it stopped, and the door opened again.

"Now, *this* is my room," said Zack, smiling. He stepped into the bedroom.

The walls were green. So were the carpet and curtains.

Most things in the room were green. Green was Zack's favorite color.

Zack spotted a huge desk. A computer touchpad was built into the desktop. The entire wall in front of it was a giant view screen.

"That's awfully big for a computer monitor," Zack said. He touched the screen. Suddenly he was looking at a HELLO, ZACK message, then zillions of stars in space. "Wow! This is so cool!" he said. "I can see the whole galaxy!"

Zack searched the stars and planets around Nebulon for a few minutes.
Then he looked around the room.

"Hey," Zack said. "Where's my
bed?"

"Are you ready for bed,
Master Just Zack?" Ira
asked.

Zack jumped at
the sound of his
voice.

"Are you in here,
too, Ira?" Zack asked.

"I am wired throughout the house,"
Ira explained. "Here is your bed."

A panel in the ceiling opened and a bed came down from above. The bed had a pillow with a matching green pillowcase and blanket.

"Cool!" Zack said. "Thanks, Ira. But it's too early for bed."

"Very well," Ira said. The bed went back into the ceiling.

"You mean I don't have to make my bed every morning?" asked Zack. "Sweet!"

"Zack, honey," called Mom through the commu-link. "Dinnertime."

Zack scooted into the elevator and rode to the dining room. He took a seat at a table that floated in midair. Charlotte and Cathy sat across from him. Mom and Dad sat on either side.

"So, Mom, what's for dinner?" Zack asked. "Are we going out?"

"No need," said Dad. A big, cheery smile spread across his face. He turned to the twins. "Girls, what would you like for dinner?"

"Spaghetti!" they both shouted.

"You got it! Zack?"

"I want a pepperoni pizza," Zack replied.

"No problem," said Dad. "Your mother and I will have grilled salmon with baked potatoes."

"Where are we going to get all that, Dad?" Zack asked.

"Right here! Ira, two spaghetti dinners, one pepperoni pizza, and two plates of grilled salmon with baked potatoes."

"Right away, Mr. Nelson," said Ira.

"Ira cooks, too?" Zack wondered aloud.

A panel in the ceiling slid open. Five plates of steaming hot food floated down and landed on the table.

Zack pulled a slice of pizza from

the pie. It had crispy star-shaped pepperoni slices that floated on top of the
gooey cheese. As Zack took his first
bite he suddenly realized just how
hungry he was.

"Wow!" said Zack. "This pizza
is great. It tastes just like the
pizza at Tip-Top Pizza
back on Earth! You
know, I think living
on Nebulon might
not be that bad
after all."

"I'm so glad,
honey," Mom said.

"After dinner we can make sure that you and your sisters are all ready for tomorrow."

"Tomorrow?" Zack asked through a mouthful of pizza.

"Yes. We've registered you at Sprockets Academy," Mom explained. "Tomorrow you start school on Nebulon."

*School!* Zack thought. He stopped chewing his pizza. Zack remembered his nightmare about school, and his monster classmates and two-headed snake teacher. *I forgot all about school!*

# Chapter 6
# Ready?
# Set?
# School!

Zack went to bed after dinner. He tossed and turned for most of the night.

*What if nobody at school likes me?* he worried. *What if they think that people from Earth are weird? I wish Bert were here.*

After staring at the ceiling for hours,

Zack finally fell into a deep sleep.

The next morning a strangely familiar voice woke him up.

"Good morning, Master Just Zack. It
is time to get ready for school."

Zack sat upright in bed. "Ira, is that you?" he asked, rubbing the sleep from his eyes.

"Yes. It is six a.m. galactic standard time. You set the alarm for that time," Ira said.

"Yeah, but I didn't expect *you* to wake me up," Zack explained. "Back on Earth, my alarm clock played my favorite song to wake me up."

"What is your favorite song?" asked Ira.

"Oh, Ira, I don't think you'd know it," Zack said. "It's called 'Rockin' Round the Stars.' It's by an Earth band called—"

"Retro Rocket," Ira said. "It was released in 2117."

Suddenly the song came blasting into Zack's room.

"You know 'Rockin' Round the Stars'?" Zack cried.

"Certainly. My memory banks contain more than six million songs from twenty-three different planets."

"Cool. Can you wake me up with that song from now on?"

"Of course," Ira replied. "Now hurry. You will be late for school."

Zack rushed into the bathroom and stepped into the shower. "Now what?"

A blast of water startled Zack.

"YA!" cried Zack. "It's too cold!"

"Adjusting," said Ira.

The water quickly became just the right temperature.

"Shall I save that shower setting for you?" Ira asked.

"You do everything, don't you?"

"Yes, I do," replied Ira.

Zack got dressed and zoomed to the kitchen. He ate toast with boingoberry  jam, which was made from a berry that grew on Venus.

"Okay, everybody, have a great day!" Dad said.

"I have an early meeting with Fred Stevens. I'll be driving the red Nebulonics car. Bye!"

After Dad left, Mom hurried Zack and the twins into the green car.

"Are you sure you know how to work this thing, Mom?" asked Zack.

"Dad showed me," Mom replied. "I just push this button and say 'Sprockets Academy.'"

As soon as she did that, the car
zoomed into the air.

When they arrived at Sprockets
Academy, a Nebulite man stepped

up to the car to greet them. "Welcome to Sprockets Academy," he said. "My name is Mr. Spudnik. I am the principal."

"Nice to meet you," said Mom. "This is Zack, Cathy, and Charlotte." The three kids got out of the car.

"Cathy and Charlotte will be in phase five," Mr. Spudnik explained. "And Zack will be in phase two. I will show you the way."

"Bye, kids!" Mom shouted as Zack and the twins followed Mr. Spudnik. "Have a great day!"

They dropped off Charlotte and Cathy at their classroom. Then Mr. Spudnik and Zack reached Zack's classroom.

"Ms. Rudolph, this is Zack Nelson. His family just moved to Nebulon from Earth," Mr. Spudnik said. "Zack, this is your teacher, Ms. Rudolph."

"Welcome, Zack," Ms. Rudolph said. "You know, I'm from Earth too."

"You are?" Zack asked.

"I moved to Nebulon about a year ago," Ms. Rudolph explained. "At first I missed Earth terribly. But now I can't imagine living anywhere but Nebulon. I think in time you'll feel the same way."

Zack found a seat and sat down. *Ms. Rudolph seems really nice*, Zack thought. *And Nebulites speak English. That'll make things a little easier.*

"Class, I would like you all to meet Zack Nelson," Ms. Rudolph said.

The students turned to face Zack. Every eye in the room was staring right at him.

# Chapter 7
# Yippee Wah-Wah!

"Hi!" said Zack. Then he raised his hand and moved it in a circle—just like his dad had done at the spaceport. The other students just stared.

"Okay, class, let's begin with today's history lesson," Ms. Rudolph said. She sat and then began typing.

Zack stared at the small screen in front of him.

*How do I get this thing to work?* he wondered.

A Nebulite boy sitting next to Zack leaned over. "Just tap the center of the screen," the boy whispered.

"Thanks," Zack whispered back. He tapped his screen and the lesson appeared.

Zack enjoyed learning about the history of Nebulon.

After history they studied math and science.

Then the bell rang for lunch, and everyone dashed from the classroom.

The students boarded a space bus to take them from the classroom to the cafeteria.

Zack stepped onto the bus. He saw
kids talking and laughing. Zack felt
like he was all alone.

*What I am doing here?* he thought. *I
want to go home.*

"Hey, Zack. There is a seat over
here," someone called out.

Zack looked toward the back of the

bus. He saw the Nebulite boy who sat next to him in class. Zack hurried down the aisle and sat next to the boy.

"I am Drake Taylor," the boy said, raising his hand and moving it in a circle.

"Nice to meet you," Zack said, doing the same hand movement.

The bus zoomed off from its dock outside the classroom building.

"How long has your family been living on Nebulon, Zack?" asked Drake.

Zack looked down at his Galactic Standard watch. "Hmm . . . about eighteen hours," Zack replied, smiling.

"How do you like it so far?" Drake asked.

"Parts of it are cool," said Zack. The last thing Zack wanted to do was to tell Drake how much he missed home.

The space bus slowed to a stop. The doors slid open, and everyone ran into the cafeteria.

Zack took a seat next to Drake and looked around.

"Hey—where's the lunch line?" Zack asked. "Where's all the food?"

"You will see," Drake replied.

Just then a line of robots came marching through the door. They were tall, skinny, and metal. Each of them pushed a cart filled with food.

A robot walked over to Zack and Drake. Zack read the choices. "I'll have super mac and cheese," he said.

The robot picked up a steaming plate of food. It set the plate down right in front of Zack.

"And I will have the jammin' jelly sandwich, please," Drake said. After Drake got his food, the boys began to eat.

"So, Zack, what did you do for fun on Earth?"

"I really liked going bike riding with my friend Bert," Zack replied.

"I, too, like to ride my bike," Drake said. "Maybe we could ride our bikes together."

"Yeah . . . okay," Zack said.

"How about we ride together today after school?" Drake asked.

"Um . . . all right."

When lunch was over, the space bus arrived to take

everyone back to class. Zack and Drake took their seats.

"Yippee wah-wah," Drake said. "My favorite class is next."

Zack stared at his new friend. "I have two questions, Drake," said Zack. "What's your favorite class? And what does 'yippee wah-wah' mean?"

Drake laughed. Zack started laughing too.

"Planetology is my favorite class," Drake replied. "And 'yippee wah-wah' is what

Nebulite kids say when they are happy."

"I love studying planets and stars too," said Zack. He was happy that he met Drake. *Looks like I made a new friend,* he thought.

# Chapter 8
# Zoom! Zoom!

The rest of Zack's school day flew right by. He really liked planetology. He learned about planets and stars he had never even heard of on Earth.

When school was over, Zack's mom arrived to pick him up. Zack walked over to the car with Drake. Charlotte

and Cathy were already inside.

"Mom, this is my new friend, Drake,"
Zack said.

"Hello, Drake," Mom said. "Very
nice to meet you."

"And these are my sisters, Charlotte
and Cathy," Zack said.

"Hello," Drake said.

"Hi . . ."

". . . Drake. . . ."

"Nice to . . ."

". . . meet you," the twins said.

"Do they talk like that all the time?"

Drake whispered.

"All the time," Zack whispered back.

Zack got into the car. "Drake's coming over later to go bike riding," he said.

"That sounds like fun," Mom said. "We'll see you later, Drake."

"We're home!" Mom announced as the car pulled into the garage.

Zack was so excited about going bike riding. He jumped out of the car and pulled his bike out from a corner of the garage.

As he got onto his bike, Zack saw something speeding toward the house.

"That looks like Drake, but what's he riding?" Zack wondered aloud.

Drake rode up to Zack. He was riding a bike.

But Zack had never seen a bike like this one. Drake's bike flew just above the ground, and it went faster than any bike Zack had ever ridden.

"Wow!" Zack cried. "What kind of bike is that?"

Drake looked puzzled. "It is just a regular Nebulon bike," he said. "Wow, you have a really old bike, Zack."

"No, it's not old,"

Zack said. "I got it for my birthday last year."

Drake just shrugged. "Come on. Time to ride."

Drake sped off on his bike. Zack pedaled hard. He tried to keep up, but his bike was not fast enough. Drake saw how far behind Zack was and hurried back.

"Would you like to try my bike?"
Drake asked.

"Sure!" Zack said.

Zack climbed onto Drake's bike. It
felt just like a regular bike.

"Just hold on tight and press that
button on the handlebars," explained
Drake. "I will ride your bike."

Zack pressed the button. He sped
along just above the ground.

"This is so cool!" Zack shouted. "I have to get one of these!"

Zack looked back and saw Drake. He was pedaling Zack's bike and smiling. Drake was far away, so Zack turned around and rode back to his friend. As they rode back to the house, Zack daydreamed about zooming around on his own Nebulon bike.

# Chapter 9
# Surprise!

Dad arrived home as Zack pulled up in front of the house. Dad reached into the back of the car and took out a big box with a bright green bow.

"Have I got a surprise for you, buddy," said Dad.

"Hi, Dad. This is my friend Drake."

"Hello, Drake. I think you'll like this too," Dad said.

*Maybe Dad got me a Nebulon bike!* thought Zack.

But then Zack heard barking from inside the box. He quickly pulled the lid off. Out jumped Zack's dog, Luna.

"Luna!" Zack shouted. "I didn't think I'd see you so soon!"

Dad smiled. "I knew how much

114

you missed her, so I put Luna on the
next cruiser to Nebulon."

"Thanks, Dad," said Zack.

Luna jumped on Zack and licked his
face. Then she jumped up on Drake.
She almost knocked him over.

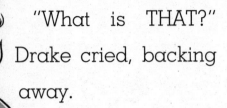

"What is THAT?" Drake cried, backing away.

"Don't be scared," Zack said. "It's just my dog, Luna. She's very friendly. Do you have a dog?"

"I have never seen a real dog before," Drake explained.

"Don't they have any dogs on Nebulon?" asked Zack.

"No," said Drake. "I think I saw a picture once, in a book."

"Well, here's something else they don't have on Nebulon," Dad said. He reached into the big box and pulled out two candy bars.

"Chocolate Nutty Crunchy Gooey Bars!" Zack said. "My favorite!"

Dad handed one candy bar to Zack and one to Drake. Both boys started munching on the treat.

"Yumzers!" Drake cried.

Zack laughed.

"That's what we say on Nebulon when something tastes really, really, really good!" explained Drake.

"Yumzers!" Zack repeated.

At that moment Mom, Charlotte, and Cathy joined the others outside.

"It's official," Mom announced. "I've decided to open a boutique. I'm going to sell Earth clothing to the women of Nebulon."

"Great idea, honey," Dad said.

"Yay!" Charlotte and Cathy both cheered.

Then Zack's hyperphone began to buzz. He pulled it from his pocket.

"Hi, Bert!" Zack said when the video chat connected. Bert's face popped up on the small screen. "Thanks for watching Luna. She just got here."

"Cool," Bert said. "I wanted to make sure she got there okay."

"How's life back on Earth?" Zack asked.

"Pretty good," Bert replied. "The Explorers Club went on a field trip to Calypso. It was fun."

"That's so cool! I hope my new school has an Explorers Club too," Zack said.

"Do you like living on Nebulon?" Bert asked.

Zack looked at his family. Then he looked at Drake and smiled. "I miss Earth," he said to Bert. "But I think I'm going to like living on Nebulon."

# GALAXY ZACK

## JOURNEY TO JUNO

# CONTENTS

# Chapter 1
# Play Ball!

Zack Nelson and his friend Drake Taylor sat in the home stadium of the Creston City Comets. A bright orange field spread out below them.

"Okay, Drake," Zack said. "I know I'm still the new kid on Nebulon. And I've never seen a galactic blast game before, but I have one question: Where are the players?"

Drake smiled and pointed to both sides of the field.

Zack looked down and saw two teams of robots. Suddenly a whistle blew, and all the robots scrambled out onto the field.

"So people don't play galactic blast? Robots do?" Zack asked.

"The robots pitch and hit and run and field," explained Drake. "But people operate the robots using remote control units."

The game began. Zack was thrilled to see that galactic blast was played just like baseball back on Earth. He instantly understood the game.

A robot batter smacked the ball deep into the outfield. A robot outfielder made a diving catch.

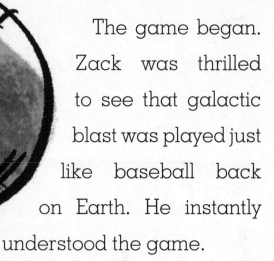

"This is so cool," said Zack. "I've got to tell my friend Bert about this. We used to watch baseball together all the time back on Earth."

"Zack, would you like to share a bag of roasted nebu-nuts?" Drake asked. "They are my favorite snack at a galactic blast game. They are very crunchy."

"Sure!" Zack exclaimed. "My treat!"

Zack got up from his seat and hurried to the snack stand. He bought a big bag of roasted nebu-nuts.

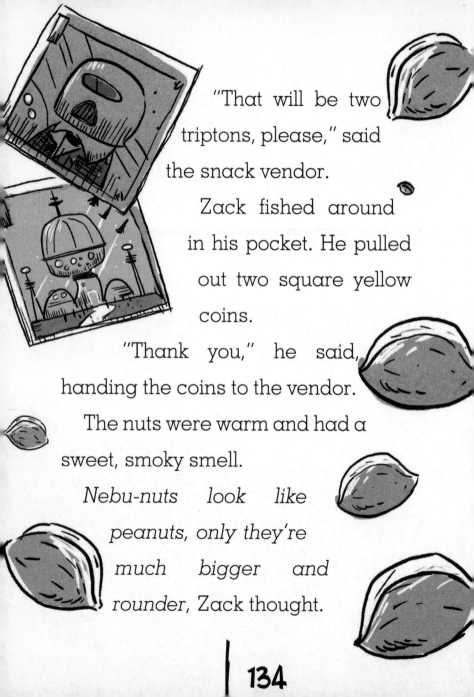

"That will be two triptons, please," said the snack vendor.

Zack fished around in his pocket. He pulled out two square yellow coins.

"Thank you," he said, handing the coins to the vendor.

The nuts were warm and had a sweet, smoky smell.

*Nebu-nuts look like peanuts, only they're much bigger and rounder,* Zack thought.

When Zack returned to his seat, he was surprised to find another boy sitting there. Zack recognized the boy from his class. He was a Sprockets student named Seth Stevens.

"Oh, hi, Seth," Zack said. "You're sitting in my seat."

"Oh yeah, well it is *my* seat now!" Seth shouted.

"But I was sitting there first," argued Zack.

"Well, I am sitting here *now*, wimpy Earthling!" Seth shot back.

"Come on, Zack," Drake said as he stood up. "Let us go and find other seats. I think I see some open seats by your dad."

*What a bully*, Zack thought. He followed Drake.

Zack and Drake found two empty seats a few rows away. Zack's dad was sitting nearby with some of his Nebulite friends. Dad smiled and waved at Zack and Drake.

"What's Seth's problem?" asked Zack as he sat down.

"Seth is the phase-two class bully," Drake explained. Phase two was Zack and Drake's grade in school. "He likes to give kids a hard time. Especially new kids."

*Great*, thought Zack. *That's just what I need.*

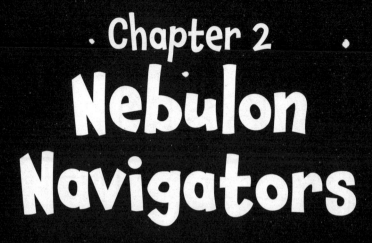

# Chapter 2
# Nebulon Navigators

The next day Zack floated through space. Whenever he saw a cool-looking planet, he dropped down for a visit.

One planet had giant trees that were more than a mile tall. Another planet had waterfalls that fell up, not down. Zack wished he could visit

every single planet in the galaxy.

"Zack?" said a soft voice that came drifting through space. "Zack Nelson?" the voice said, a little louder this time. "Can you please tell the class the answer to problem number seven?"

Zack looked up and realized that he was not in space at all. He was sitting in school, in Ms. Rudolph's class at Sprockets Academy. He had been daydreaming.

Zack scratched his head. "Forty-two?" he replied hopefully.

The whole class giggled.

"Zack, we are studying grammar at the moment, not math," Ms. Rudolph explained. "Please pay attention."

The rest of the morning dragged for Zack. Just before the sonic recess bell chimed, Ms. Rudolph made an announcement.

"Don't forget, the Sprockets Academy Explorers Club is going on a very special trip this week," she began. "The club will be going to Juno. It's not too late to sign up."

*Wow!* Zack thought. He had been reading all about Juno in the Space and Science section of the *Nebulon News*—the planet's online holographic newspaper. Juno had just been discovered. Zack really wanted to go there.

"Students who go on the trip will be helping the Nebulon Navigators explore this new planet," Ms. Rudolph explained.

Zack then slipped into another daydream. This time he was exploring Juno. He stepped into a cave and found pieces of old pottery.

"There must have been life here thousands of years ago," Explorer Zack announced to the scientists.

"Zack, this is the most amazing discovery ever," said the head of the Nebulon Navigators. "You will be famous!"

Zack imagined a series of z-mail news blasts. Each one had a giant headline:

ZACK NELSON MAKES MOST IMPORTANT DISCOVERY EVER!

ZACK NELSON INVITED TO JOIN NEBULON NAVIGATORS!

ZACK NELSON, BOY GENIUS!

The sonic recess bell suddenly chimed, and Zack snapped out of his daydream.

"Permission slips are up on the school's Sprocketsphere site.

Please have your parents sign them and zap them back to me," said Ms. Rudolph.

Everyone quickly rushed out of the classroom.

"Who are the Nebulon Navigators?" Zack whispered to Drake.

"They are the most famous space scientists on Nebulon," Drake explained. "They explore other planets."

"Cool," replied Zack. "I really want to go to Juno."

"Great," Drake said. "I am a member of the Sprockets Explorers Club. You should join."

"I will. That way we can explore the galaxy together and make great discoveries," said Zack.

"Not if I make them first, Earth wimp!" said Seth Stevens. Seth pushed past Zack and ran out into the play zone for recess.

# Chapter 3
# Torkus Dorkus

Zack and Drake stood just outside the play zone.

"Why does Seth have to do stuff like that?" Zack asked. "Why does he have to call me names? I can't help it if I'm not from Nebulon."

"Try not to let it bother you, Zack,"

Drake said. "Seth thinks he is better than everyone else."

"Why?" asked Zack.

"His father works at Nebulonics," Drake explained.

"But, so does mine," Zack pointed out.

"Yes, but Seth's dad invented the Torkus Magnus, the fastest bike on Nebulon."

"Torkus DORKus," mumbled Zack.

"What did you say?" asked Drake.

"Uh, never mind," said Zack. "So, is it even faster than *your* bike?" Zack had ridden Drake's cool super-fast Nebulon bike the day they met.

"Twice as fast!" Drake replied. "It will not even be in the stores until sometime next year. Of course, Seth already has one."

"That's still no reason to be so mean," Zack said.

Zack and Drake stood in line for the simulon course. The course was the most popular recess activity.

None of the hoops, ladders, hurdles, or barriers were real. They were all 3-D holographic images—pictures of objects that looked just like the real thing. But that didn't make it any less fun.

Zack's turn came. He dashed down a narrow path. Then he jumped up and over a blinking fence. Dropping

to the ground, he crawled through a long, winding tube.

"Done!" shouted Zack.

"Pretty good," Drake said, looking at his Galactic Standard watch. "Twenty-two seconds."

"Big deal," snarled Seth. "I did it in eighteen seconds. You Earthlings are so slow."

Zack tried his best to ignore Seth.

# Chapter 4
# Permission Granted!

Zack took the Sprockets Speedybus home from school. He couldn't wait to tell his parents about the Explorers Club and the trip to Juno.

When he got home, Zack's dog, Luna, was there to greet him.

"Hey there, Luna!" said Zack. He

kneeled down to pet her head.

Luna licked Zack's face. Her tail wagged happily.

"I'm glad to see you too, girl," Zack said. "Come on!"

Zack's mom, Shelly Nelson, was in the garage. She was setting up the family's old barbecue grill from Earth.

"What do you need *that* for, Mom?"
Zack asked. "Can't you just ask Ira to
cook whatever you like?"

Ira was the Nelson family's Indoor
Robotic Assistant. He was part of the
electrical, mechanical, computer, and
communications systems of the entire
house. Ira cooked all the Nelsons'

meals. He also took messages, announced visitors, and made sure the temperature in the house was always comfortable.

"I thought it would be fun to show our new Nebulite friends how we made food back on Earth," Mom explained. "So your father and I are having a barbecue party this weekend."

"Sounds like fun," said Zack. He realized that it was Monday.

The journey to Juno was scheduled for Thursday. "I'll be back by then."

"Back?" Mom asked, stopping what she was doing. "Back from where?"

"From the planet Juno!" Zack exclaimed. He couldn't hide his excitement.

"There's an Explorers Club at Sprockets. They are going to Juno later this week. Can I join, Mom? Can I? Drake's going. We'll be helping the Nebulon Navigators explore Juno!"

"That's great, Zack," Mom replied. "Of course you can go. I'm very glad that you found a school club you want to join. Dad and I will download the permission form and zap it back to the school."

"Yippee wah-wah!" said Zack. Mom gave him a hug before he rushed inside. When Zack entered the kitchen, a familiar voice greeted him.

"Welcome home, Master Just Zack," Ira said immediately. When Zack first met Ira, he called Zack "Master Zack." Zack told Ira that he didn't have to call him "master"—"just Zack" was fine. Since then, Ira had called him "Master Just Zack."

Zack was used to it now. And he kind of liked it.

"Hi, Ira," replied Zack. "May I have some peanut butter cookies?"

"Certainly," said Ira.

A plate full of cookies popped out of a slot in the wall. Zack grabbed one and took a bite.

"You sure these are peanut butter cookies, Ira?" he asked.

"Actually, Master Just Zack, they are nebu-nut cookies," Ira explained. "Peanuts do not grow on Nebulon."

"These are pretty good," Zack said. "But peanut butter is my all-time fave!"

Zack grabbed a few more cookies and stepped into the elevator. The doors slid shut and he took off—sideways.

# Chapter 5
## Thoughts of Juno

The elevator sped through the house. The doors opened, and Zack stepped into his bedroom. He sat at his desk to do his homework.

But Zack couldn't concentrate.

*I'm going to Juno!*

It was all Zack could think about!

173

Zack had not been happy when he moved from Earth to Nebulon. He missed his friends. He missed familiar foods. But if the Nelsons hadn't come to Nebulon, Zack would not be going to explore Juno.

*I'll finish my homework later,* Zack thought. He ran back into the elevator and sped to the living room.

Zack flipped on the sonic cell monitor, the Nebulon version of television. He put on the galactic blast

game. The Creston City Comets were leading the Voltor Shocks 5 to 4.

A few minutes later, Zack's dad, Otto Nelson, came home from his job at Nebulonics.

"Hey, Captain!" Dad said. "How was school today?"

"Great!" Zack exclaimed. "I joined the Explorers Club. I'm going on a trip to Juno!"

"Wow! Got room for one more?" Dad joked.

Zack thought about Seth. "Dad, do you know the guy who invented the Torkus Magnus?" he asked.

"Of course! He's Fred Stevens, my boss at Nebulonics. Remember—he greeted us at the space station when we first landed on Nebulon? I'm having lunch with him tomorrow."

*Seth Stevens's dad is my dad's boss!* Zack thought. *Ugh.*

"You like him?" Zack asked.

"Sure," Dad replied. "He's a great guy. Say, isn't Fred's son in phase two at Sprockets?"

"Yeah, I think he is," Zack muttered. "You know, I haven't met all the kids yet." Zack did not want to tell his dad what a big bully Seth was.

"Hi, Dad . . . ," said Charlotte and Cathy together. Zack's twin sisters often spoke as if they were one person.

"Look at what . . . ," Charlotte began.

". . . we got!" Cathy finished.

They squealed with delight. They
held up identical pink dresses that had
been sent from Earth.

"These are . . ."

". . . the coolest dresses ever!"

Then they ran off to their room to try
the new dresses on.

Mom walked in with some laundry. "Hurry up, girls," she called after the twins. "It's almost time for dinner."

Zack and Dad went to watch the rest of the Comets game together, but only one thought filled Zack's mind.

*I'm going to Juno!*

# Chapter 6

# Juno Bound

Zack stood in front of Sprockets Academy. He wore his Explorers Club hat and his spacepack. Today he was going to Juno!

The rest of the club was gathered outside the school. Zack spotted Seth Stevens. Seth was the last person Zack hoped would be on this trip. Then he saw Drake.

"Drake, over here!" Zack called. Drake joined him.

"I cannot believe we are actually going to Juno," said Drake. "Only a handful of people have ever seen it."

A man stepped to the front of the crowd. He was tall and had a skinny green head. He had six long fingers on each hand.

On top of his thin head was a galactic blast cap that read DREXEL EXPLORERS CLUB EARTH JOURNEY 2098. Clearly this man was neither a Nebulite nor a human.

185

"Welcome, explorers!" he began. "I am Mr. Shecky, the adviser of the Sprockets Explorers Club. I'll be your leader on your journey to Juno. Now please follow me onto the space cruiser."

Zack, Drake, and the rest of the explorers piled onto a jumbo space cruiser.

A few moments later they took off into space.

Zack walked to a window to watch stars and comets streaking by.

"Hey—you're Zack, right?" asked Mr. Shecky, standing next to Zack.

Zack nodded.

"Ms. Rudolph told me about you," Mr. Shecky said. "She said that you're from Earth, and that you're new on Nebulon. Well, I'm from the planet Drexel myself. I know what it's like to be the new kid."

Zack pointed at Mr. Shecky's cap. "You've been to Earth?" he asked.

"Yup. I used to be a galaxy researcher," Mr. Shecky explained. "I was on the Drexel Deep Space Team. I love exploring planets. I moved to Nebulon to become the adviser for the Sprockets Academy Explorers Club."

Zack settled back into his seat and thought about the adventure ahead.

A short while later the cruiser began beeping. Everyone leaned forward.

"Attention, please. Arrival on Juno in five minutes. Prepare for landing," the cruiser said.

Zack looked out the window. He saw a craggy-looking planet that sparkled.

Juno looked as if it were covered in diamonds.

*This is it!* Zack thought.

The cruiser landed gently on the surface of Juno. The hatch opened and everyone stepped out. A sparkling crystal landscape stretched out before them.

Zack saw lots of space cruisers from other schools. They came from different

planets, such as Zorba, Neptune, Cylon, and more.

Then Zack spotted the Nebulon Navigators team. They were already hard at work gathering samples.

"Wow! I can't believe I'm here with the Nebulon Navigators," Zack said to Drake.

"Welcome to Juno, everyone," Mr. Shecky announced. "Each school's Explorers Club has been assigned a section of Juno. Sprockets Academy will explore the southwest quadrant. Over there."

Mr. Shecky pointed to a series of caves in the distance.

"I'm going to break you into teams," said Mr. Shecky. "Everyone will work with a partner."

*I hope Drake and I can be partners!* thought Zack.

"You are to take notes, gather samples, record videos, and shoot photos with your team's handheld camtrams," Mr. Shecky continued.

Mr. Shecky began reading aloud pairs of names. When he got to Zack's name, Zack held his breath.

"'Zack Nelson and Seth Stevens!'" Mr. Shecky called out.

*Oh no!* Zack thought. *Not him!* He had a sinking feeling in the pit of his stomach.

# Chapter 7
# Crystal Caves

Zack and Seth set off for the crystal caves. *Okay, I'm not going to let Seth Stevens ruin my chance to explore Juno,* Zack thought.

Zack paused at the entrance to the first cave. He turned on his camtram and began recording. "This cave appears to be surrounded by a ring of flickering rocks," Zack reported. "It looks like they have tiny blinking lights inside them. Pretty cool, huh, Seth?" He figured he would at least try to get along with Seth.

But Seth had his face buried in his hyperphone.

"Yeah, yeah, whatever," mumbled Seth.

They stepped into the cave. The light from the camtram helped them see. Zack saw crystals of all shapes and sizes.

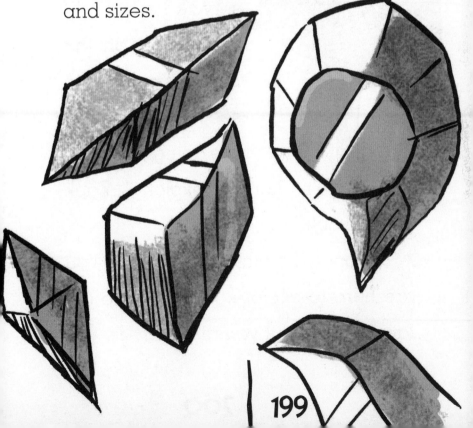

"Oh great!" Seth whined. "What kind of a dumb planet is this anyway? I can-not even get z-mail service here. And I cannot get on the Sprocketsphere to see what my friends are doing."

"But we're here to explore," Zack pointed out.

"Wrong!" Seth snapped. "*You* are here to explore. *I* am here to get famous for what you discover. So you better find something special."

Zack just shook his head.

"Hey, Earth wimp, get a picture of that!" shouted Seth. He pointed at a large crystal right over their heads.

Zack glanced up and saw what
looked like an octopus hanging from
the ceiling. He aimed the camtram
and took a picture.

Zack and Seth walked deeper into
the cave. They soon came to a river
flowing through the icy crystal floor.

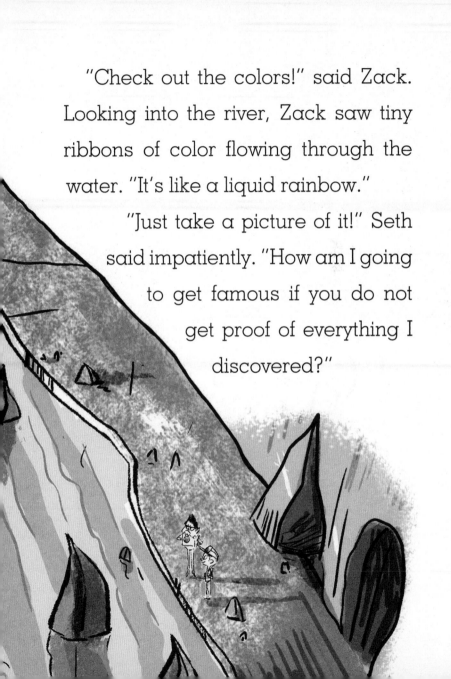

"Check out the colors!" said Zack. Looking into the river, Zack saw tiny ribbons of color flowing through the water. "It's like a liquid rainbow."

"Just take a picture of it!" Seth said impatiently. "How am I going to get famous if you do not get proof of everything I discovered?"

*Part of me doesn't even want to record any more discoveries, Zack* thought. *Not if Seth is going to take all the credit when I'm doing all the work.*

"Why did you join the Explorers Club if you aren't even interested in exploring?" Zack asked Seth.

Seth shrugged. "My dad made me. He said it would look good on my student record."

Zack sighed. He pointed the camtram at the river and started recording it.

"All the colors of the rainbow seem to flow through this river," he said.

"Because we're in a cave, the colors can't be formed by sunlight. They are already in the water."

Seth quickly lost interest in what Zack was doing. He wandered over to the entrance of the cave. Then he pulled out his hyperphone and tried again to get a signal.

Zack hiked deeper into the cave. He went around a bend and found a pile of crystals.

Zack picked up one of the crystals. It felt smooth and cold.

Suddenly, Zack felt a wave of warm energy wash over him.

"Whoa. That heat is coming from the pile of crystals," Zack said.

He spotted a soft green glow coming from the pile. Zack moved a few crystals out of the way.

"It's a glowing green crystal!" he said. Then he quickly looked back over his shoulder to see if Seth was there.

Zack picked up the green crystal. Unlike the others, this one was warm. It was about the size of a baseball.

Zack opened his spacepack and slipped the crystal in.

"Seth is *not* going to take credit for this one!"

# Chapter 8
# An Amazing Discovery

Zack hurried back toward the cave entrance.

*I'll show the green crystal to the other Explorers Clubs,* he thought. *And maybe even to the Nebulon Navigators. I'll be famous!*

Once again Zack imagined a series

of news blasts. In his mind, giant z-mail headlines flooded Nebulon:

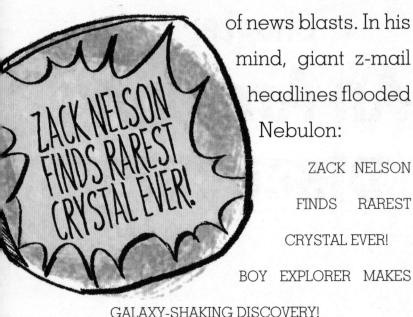

ZACK NELSON FINDS RAREST CRYSTAL EVER!

BOY EXPLORER MAKES GALAXY-SHAKING DISCOVERY!

ZACK NELSON AWARDED THE ZURBIC PRIZE FOR SCIENCE!

Zack rejoined Seth outside the cave.

"Come on!" said Seth. "There are more great

ZACK NELSON AWARDED THE ZURBIC PRIZE FOR SCIENCE!

discoveries for me to make."

Zack spent a few more hours recording interesting crystal and water formations. Seth spent the time complaining and pacing around. Then the two rejoined the rest of the Sprockets students.

Zack saw many students from different Explorers Clubs. They were all eagerly sharing the exciting discoveries they had made.

Seth grabbed the camtram right out of Zack's hands.

"Hey, everyone, check out all the grape stuff I found," said Seth.

"Grape?" Zack whispered to Drake.

"On Nebulon, we call awesome stuff 'grape,'" Drake explained. "It is like when people on Earth say 'cool.'"

Seth played back the video and photos of all the discoveries that Zack had made. Everyone oohed and aahed as Seth took credit for all of Zack's hard work.

*That's it!* Zack thought. *I've had enough of Seth.*

"Thank you, Seth," said Mr. Shecky. "Excellent work."

Then Zack pulled the green crystal from his spacepack. It glowed and pulsed with warm energy.

"Mr. Shecky, I also found this," Zack announced.

Mr. Shecky's eyes opened wide.

"Zack, where did you find this?" He gasped. "Do you know what this is?"

"No, I don't," Zack replied.

Seth glared at Zack.

"That, young man, is a galaxy gemmite!" exclaimed Mr. Shecky. "That crystal has an incredible amount of energy stored within it. Usually they're the size of pebbles.

But a gemmite this size could power all of Creston City for a whole year. A gemmite this large hasn't been found in more than one hundred years!"

Seth clenched his fists. His face turned bright red.

Zack smiled. *Maybe now more kids will like me*, he thought.

A researcher from the Nebulon Navigators hurried over to the Sprockets group.

"What is all the fuss about, Mr. Shecky?" the researcher asked.

Zack held up the gemmite.

"Why, that is amazing!" said the researcher. "You found that?"

Zack nodded.

"No fair!" cried one of the Explorers Club members.

"Yeah!" shouted another member. "We have all been in the Explorers Club longer than Zack. We have been on lots more trips. We never found anything like that!"

*Oh no!* Zack thought. *This is not what I wanted to happen!*

As the excitement increased, more Explorers Clubs came over to see what was going on. So did the rest of the Nebulon Navigators.

"A huge gemmite!" exclaimed one of the Navigators. "Who found this?"

Zack stepped forward.

"The students of the Sprockets Academy Explorers Club found it," Zack announced. "We make a great team!"

Everyone in the club cheered. They all surrounded Zack and patted him on the back.

Everyone except Seth, who looked on from a distance.

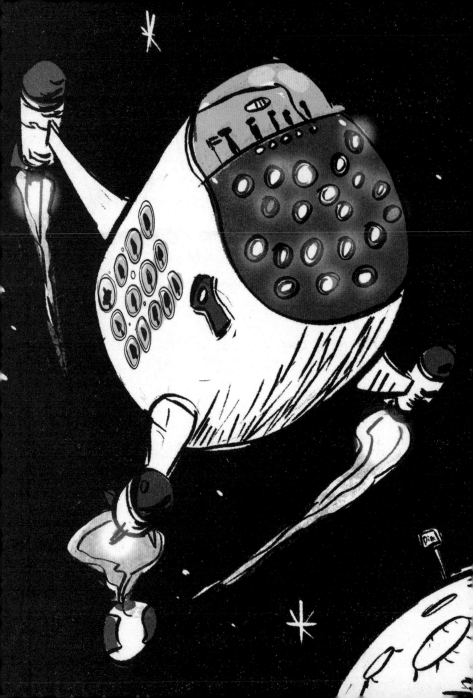

# Chapter 9
# Fame and Friendship

Zack had a great time on the trip back to Nebulon. Everyone on the space cruiser was in a fantastic mood.

The Explorers Club was proud of the incredible discovery they had made. And they were happy that Zack shared the credit with everyone.

Zack finally began to feel like he belonged on Nebulon.

When he got home, Zack was shocked to see how fast the news of his discovery had spread. Z-mail blasts were everywhere showing the Sprockets Explorers Club holding the gemmite. Zack was up front in all the photos.

Zack and his family gathered in the living room. He flipped on the sonic cell

monitor. The *Evening Galactic News* came on.

"Good evening. A group of students from Nebulon has made an amazing discovery," the newscaster said. "The Explorers Club of Sprockets Academy found the largest gemmite anyone has seen in years."

Charlotte and Cathy both pointed at
the screen.

"Look . . ."

". . . it's Zack!" they both said.

"We're very proud of you, Zack,"
said Dad. "You're a natural explorer!"

Zack's mom watched all the kids on Juno celebrating with Zack.

"And it looks like you made some new friends," said Mom.

Just then Zack's video-chat hyperphone started buzzing. He looked at the screen.

"It's Bert calling from Earth," Zack said. "I'll be in my room!"

"Go ahead, Captain," said Dad. "We'll just watch you on the sonic cell monitor!"

229

Zack hurried to his room. He plugged the hyperphone into his 3-D holocam.

Instantly a life-size 3-D image of Bert appeared in his room.

"Dude, I just saw you on TV," Bert said. "You're famous!"

Zack was still amazed at how lifelike the image of his friend was. It felt like Bert was right there hanging out in his room—just like in the old days back on Earth.

"It was pretty grape finding that gemmite," admitted Zack.

"'Grape'?" asked Bert. "Are you hungry?"

"No!" Zack laughed. "Sorry—that's what they say on Nebulon when something is cool," he explained.

"Sounds like you're fitting right in there," said Bert.

"I'm doing okay," Zack said. "But I still

miss hanging out with you."

Zack went to pat Bert on the back. But no matter how lifelike the image of Bert was, it still was not the real thing. His hand passed right through the 3-D image of his friend!

"Whoa, dude. That is just *too* creepy!" said Zack.

# Chapter 10

# Burgers and Dogs

A couple of days later the Nelsons held their old-fashioned Earth-style barbecue. They had invited all their new Nebulite friends.

Zack and the girls helped Mom carry platters of uncooked burgers, hot dogs, chicken, corn on the cob,

and vegetables out to the backyard.

"Hey, look what we got!" shouted Dad. He ran from the house holding an open package. "Real peanut butter cookies, made with real peanuts!"

"Wow!" exclaimed Zack. "Where'd these come from?"

"Bert's mom made them," Dad said. "Bert told her how much you missed real peanut butter cookies—"

"Excuse me, Mr. Nelson," Ira said. "Some of your guests have arrived."

A few minutes later a crowd of
Nebulites gathered in the backyard.
Zack didn't know the adults, but he
recognized most of the kids from
school.

And of course Drake was there. The
kids all gathered around the barbecue
grill.

"Yow! What are those burning round things?" Drake asked.

"Those are burgers," explained Zack. "They're yumzers!"

"Mr. Stevens and his family have arrived," Ira announced.

Dad's boss, Fred Stevens, walked into the backyard. He was followed by

his wife, Angie, and their son, Seth.

*Seth Stevens!* Zack thought. *Here in my yard? I guess I should be polite since he's my guest.*

Zack walked up to Seth.

"Hi, Seth. Glad you made it. Would you like some food?"

Just then Luna ran over. She jumped up onto Seth.

"Yah!" Seth cried, backing away in fear.

Zack was surprised to see Seth so scared. Despite all the bullying, Zack actually felt sorry for Seth.

Zack remembered how frightened
Drake had been the first time he met
Luna.

"Luna's friendly," Zack told Seth.
"She won't hurt you. She's my dog."

Seth joined the other kids over near
the food.

"Would you like a hot dog?" Zack
offered.

"You eat dogs?" Seth said. "But I thought you liked Luna."

"Hot dogs aren't made from dogs," Zack explained. "That's their name."

"Weird," said Seth.

"Would anyone . . ."

". . . like to . . ."

". . . dance?" Charlotte and Cathy asked.

The Nebulites looked puzzled.

"You know . . . dancing," added Zack's mom.

"Ira, how about a little dance music?" Zack's dad said.

"Certainly, Mr. Nelson," said Ira.

Loud dance music blared out into the backyard.

Zack's dad and mom started to dance. Their Nebulite guests just stared at them. Music and dancing were not popular on Nebulon.

Mr. Shecky joined right in. "I love music!" he said. "Come on, everybody. It's fun!"

Slowly a few Nebulites joined in. They imitated the moves that Zack's dad and mom were making.

Zack turned away, trying not to giggle. He glanced over at all his new Nebulite friends. He thought about his adventure on Juno. Seth wasn't even bothering him today! He smiled and looked up into the pink Nebulon sky.

248

That's when Zack saw something streak across the sky.

*What is that?* Zack wondered.

Zack rushed inside. He hurried to his room and flipped on his überzoom galactic telescope. He zoomed in on the streak. Now he could clearly see a body and wings. Zack could not believe his eyes.

# GALAXY ZACK

## THE PREHISTORIC PLANET

# CONTENTS

# Chapter 1
# Run for Your Life!

Zack Nelson ran through a jungle. Every tree he saw looked different. They were nothing like the trees that he knew on Earth. They were also not like any tree he had seen so far on his new home planet, Nebulon.

In the distance Zack saw a huge

waterfall. It rose hundreds of feet into the air. The water crashed into a lake below, making a sound like thunder.

Zack felt confused as he ran along a path.

*Omph!*

Zack tripped over a large white rock and landed on his

stomach. As he picked himself back up he heard a *ka-raaaaack!!!*

This noise was followed by a high-pitched screech behind him.

*Screeeeeeeee!!!*

Turning back toward the white rock, Zack discovered that it was not a rock at all. It was a huge egg. A tiny creature stepped out of the egg. It let out another ear-splitting yell.

*Screeeeeeeee!!!*

"I've seen pictures of that animal,"

Zack said to himself.
"It's a baby Tyrannosaurus
rex! They're cute when they're
small."

Suddenly, the ground began to
shake. An earth-shaking roar split the
air.

*ROOOAAAARRRRR!*

Zack looked up and saw a huge

Tyrannosaurus rex rumbling toward him.

"YAAAAA!" he shouted, running in terror. "They're not so cute when they're big!"

Zack ran through the jungle, crashing through branches and leaves. He looked back over his shoulder and saw the giant dinosaur catching up to him.

That's when he began to hear familiar music.

"Wait a minute," he said. "I know that song. It's 'Rockin' Round the Stars' by Retro Rocket. But how can it be playing here in this jungle?"

The music grew louder and louder. The dinosaur got closer and closer.

261

"Master Just Zack," said a very familiar voice. "It is time to get ready for school."

"Ira?" Zack asked.

Zack's eyes popped open. He saw that he was not in a jungle. He was in his bed, sweating from his nightmare.

Ira, the Nelson family's Indoor Robotic Assistant, was waking Zack up. He did this every morning by playing Zack's favorite song. Zack bolted from his bed, rubbed the sleep from his eyes, and thought, *I've GOT to explore the Prehistoric Planet!*

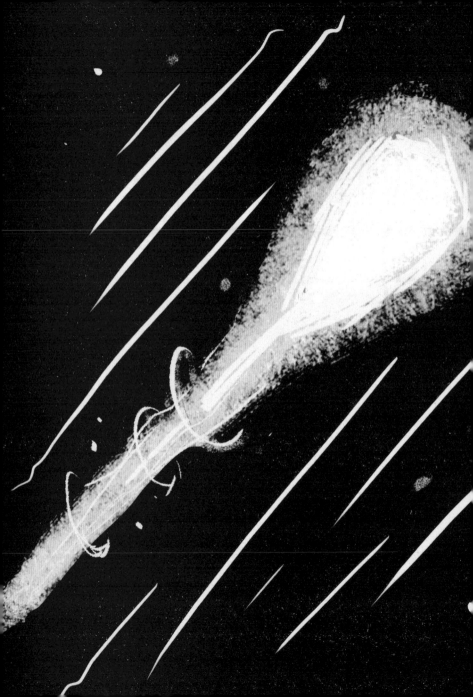

# Chapter 2

# Pterosaur Troubles

At breakfast the next morning Zack couldn't stop thinking about the real-life dinosaur that was right there on Nebulon. The week before, Zack had seen something streaking through the sky. He looked through his überzoom telescope and was amazed to see a

265

Extinct Dinosaur
Found!

creature flying through the air above Nebulon.

When the creature landed, it turned out to be a baby pterosaur—a dinosaur that had been extinct on Earth for hundreds of millions of years! News of the pterosaur spread through z-mail blasts and sonic cell news reports. Soon everyone on Nebulon and even throughout the entire galaxy knew about the creature.

OH, BABY!
Pterosaur Hits
Nebulon

Wow! Check Out This Dino!

Zack's dad, Otto Nelson, sat at the breakfast table reading the *Nebulon News*. This was the planet's online holographic newspaper. Lifelike 3-D images of the dinosaur flapping its wings in a cage jumped from the screen of his tablet reader.

"I studied pterosaurs on Earth," explained Zack. "I learned how to pronounce their name! You say it like 'TER-oh-sore.' And I learned that they look like giant birds. They have long pointy beaks. And the backs of their heads come to a point. Their wings are bigger than their skinny bodies. And they have long narrow tails."

"You do know a lot about pterosaurs, Zack," said Dad. "At least this one is safe, and the top scientists on Nebulon are taking good care of him. They're trying to build him a bigger cage for him to fly in."

"The poor thing," said Zack's mom, Shelly Nelson. "How long do you think it'll take them to find its home planet?"

"No one knows for sure, honey," Dad said. "The scientists are looking as hard as they can for the Prehistoric Planet, where the pterosaur came from. It could be days, weeks, even

years before they find the planet."

"Years?" asked Zack. "I hope it doesn't take that long."

"Poor little guy . . ."

". . . he must be . . ."

". . . so scared," said Charlotte and Cathy, Zack's twin sisters.

"Everyone at Nebulonics is working

very hard to find his home," said Dad.

Nebulonics was where Zack's dad worked. It was the best electronics research company on the planet. Nebulonics was always inventing new things to help make life easier.

"We're building an ultra-shuttle that can safely and quickly make the trip to the Prehistoric Planet. We're going

to take the poor fella home."

"That's pretty grape," said Zack. In the few months he had lived on Nebulon, Zack had gotten comfortable using the word "grape" instead of "cool."

"You bet, Captain," Dad said, getting up from the table. "Well, time for work. I'll see you all tonight."

*Captain!* Zack thought. "Captain" was what Zack's dad liked to call him.

273

But this time it made Zack imagine himself at the controls of the ultra-shuttle. He was piloting the space ship, taking the pterosaur back home.

"Hey, that reminds me," said Dad just before he reached the front door. "Tomorrow is Bring Your Child to Work Day on Earth. I asked my boss, Fred Stevens, if I could bring you to work, Zack. And even though Nebulites have

274

never heard of that tradition, Fred said yes."

Zack's eyes opened wide.

"So, do you want to come to work with me tomorrow?" Dad asked. "You'll get to see the ultra-shuttle up close!"

"You bet!" exclaimed Zack. "Thanks!"

Once again, Zack found himself dreaming about piloting the ultra-shuttle. He could think of nothing else for the rest of the day.

# Chapter 3
# Inside Nebulonics

The next morning Zack was the first one up. He was dressed and ready to go even before his dad.

"All set, Zack?" asked Dad.

"Yup! I'm taking my new camtram so I can take pictures of all the grape stuff at Nebulonics," Zack replied,

holding up his handheld device.

Zack and his dad slipped into the shiny red Nebulonics car. They sped through the sky above Creston City.

A few minutes later they landed in the conveyor lot at Nebulonics.

"This is it!" Dad said excitedly.

Zack could tell that his dad was really happy to have him there.

As soon as they stepped out of the car, a large robotic arm sprung out from a conveyor belt. It lifted the car onto the moving belt. Then the car disappeared into a storage slot where it would stay until Dad needed it at the end of the day.

Zack stepped into the Nebulonics building. He couldn't believe his eyes!

Everywhere he looked, people were busy putting things together. Some were building machines that moved on their own. Others wired up complex computer circuits.

*This place is cool! Dad is lucky to have a job like this,* Zack thought as he looked around.

Dad's boss, Fred Stevens, came over to welcome them.

"Glad you are here, Zack," said Fred. "Feel free to look around."

"Thank you, Mr. Stevens!" Zack replied.

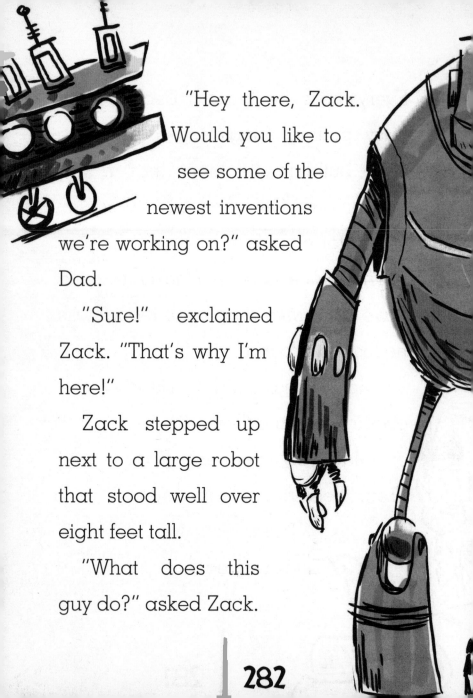

"Hey there, Zack. Would you like to see some of the newest inventions we're working on?" asked Dad.

"Sure!" exclaimed Zack. "That's why I'm here!"

Zack stepped up next to a large robot that stood well over eight feet tall.

"What does this guy do?" asked Zack.

"It's the latest model of galactic blast robot," explained Dad. "They'll be on the field next season. They're twice as fast as the current players."

"Wow!" Zack cried. "I can't wait to go to a galactic blast game next season!"

Zack couldn't be happier. He used his camtram to take photos and movies of all the amazing gadgets.

They came around a corner and Zack stopped in his tracks. There stood the coolest bicycle ever made.

"It's the Torkus Magnus!" Zack exclaimed. "I saw Seth Stevens riding one!"

Seth was Fred's son. He was also the school bully, and the only kid who had a Torkus Magnus bike.

"Why don't I take a picture of you on the bike?" asked Dad.

"Yeah!" Zack cried, handing his dad the camtram. He climbed onto the bike, which was mounted on a stand.

"Here I am riding the Torkus Magnus!" Zack said into the camtram. He pressed the buttons and turned the handlebars.

Zack didn't want to get off. Even though the bike wasn't going any-where, he loved the idea of riding it.

"Okay, c'mon, Zack," Dad said after a couple of minutes. "There's a lot more to see."

# Chapter 4
# Ultra Grape!

The tour continued. In each room Zack saw another cool gadget.

"I think you'll really like this," Dad said. He pointed to a telescope that looked a lot like the überzoom galactic telescope Zack had in his room.

"We call this the Galactic Uplink,"

explained Dad. "It's based on the überzoom telescope, of course. But this version records what you see as a video and automatically uploads it to your computer."

"This is all so cool!" Zack said.

"And now, the best part," Dad said, smiling.

They reached a large metal door. Dad took out and swiped his ID card. Then he placed his hand on a screen. The screen flashed green.

"Your turn," said Dad.

Zack put his hand up on the screen. It flashed again.

"Otto Nelson and one guest," a voice from the screen said. "You are cleared to enter."

The door slid open and they walked into a large room with a high ceiling. In the center of the room sat the ultra-shuttle.

"WHOA!" Zack exclaimed. "That's what you're building to take the pterosaur home!"

"Exactly," replied Dad. "Everyone here at Nebulonics has been working on it ever since the pterosaur landed on Nebulon. It's almost ready."

Zack turned on his camtram and took video of the shuttle from all angles.

Just then the door to the shuttle room slid open. In rushed Fred Stevens.

"Otto, have you heard the news?" Mr. Stevens asked excitedly.

"What news?" asked Dad.

"It just came across the sonic cell monitor," explained Mr. Stevens. "It looks like the Nebulon Navigators have found the Prehistoric Planet!"

293

# Chapter 5
# An Unexpected Trip

That night at dinner all Zack could talk about was the Prehistoric Planet. He had had a great day at Nebulonics, but this amazing discovery was the biggest news of the year.

"A team of scientists used a test model of the new Galactic Uplink telescope," explained Dad. "And the Nebulon Navigators used star charts they had created during their missions exploring the galaxy."

"Like the mission I went on with them to Juno!" Zack said excitedly.

"Exactly," replied Dad. "And their timing couldn't have been better. We'll have the ultra-shuttle ready soon. Then we can bring the pterosaur home."

At that moment Dad's hyperphone began to buzz.

"Excuse me," he said, pulling it from his pocket. "It's from Fred."

"He doesn't usually z-mail you at home," Zack's mom pointed out.

"It must . . ."

". . . be very . . ."

". . . important,"
Charlotte and
Cathy added.

"You said it, girls!" Dad exclaimed after he read the z-mail. "Nebulonics wants me to go on the mission to the Prehistoric Planet!"

"That is so grape, Dad!" said Zack.

"It sure is! They want an engineer on board to make sure that everything on the ultra-shuttle runs smoothly. I'm going with the scientists and the

Nebulon Navigators to take the lost pterosaur home!"

"Wow!" cried Zack. "Can I go with you? Please, Dad? Please, please, please? You know how much I love planet hopping. And I've already been on one mission with the Nebulon Navigators. And I think that dinosaurs are super-cool!"

"Uh . . . I don't know, Captain," said Dad. "I'll talk with Fred tomorrow."

After dinner, Zack took his dog, Luna, for a walk. He did this every evening. He loved talking to Luna even though she couldn't talk back. She was a good listener.

"Dad is going to take that dinosaur

home, Luna," Zack said as Luna trotted
along beside him. "And guess what?"

Luna looked up at him and tilted
her head. She looked as if she were
waiting for the answer.

"*I* may get to go too!"

*Yip! Yip!* Luna barked.

"Isn't that great?!" said Zack.

That night Zack could hardly sleep. His mind was filled with nothing but dinosaurs. He imagined the homepage of the *Nebulon News* with the headline: EARTH BOY AND NAVIGATORS SAVE BABY DINOSAUR! Next to the headline there would be a photo of Zack with the pterosaur and a group of Nebulon Navigators.

When Zack finally fell asleep, he again dreamed about running through a jungle filled with dinosaurs.

# Chapter 6
# Zack Nelson, Daydreamer

The next day at school Zack sat in Ms. Rudolph's class. He was still daydreaming about the Prehistoric Planet. He could see himself with the Nebulon Navigators, watching as the baby pterosaur was reunited with its mother.

A distant voice sounded in the jungle.

"Zack?" the voice seemed to be saying.

Then it got a bit louder. "Zack!"

Then it was *really* loud. "ZACK NELSON! Please pay attention!"

Zack snapped out of his daydream
to find Ms. Rudolph standing over him.

"I asked you a question about the
second age of Nebulon history," said
Ms. Rudolph.

"I'm sorry, Ms. Rudolph. I'll pay
attention. I promise."

During lunch Zack told his friend Drake Taylor all about the pterosaur, Nebulonics, and how he might be able to go on the trip.

"How can I think about school when I may be rocketing to the Prehistoric Planet?" asked Zack. "I can't think about anything else—not even this super-yummy galactic patty."

Drake was excited for his friend. "That would be so grape!" said Drake. He took a sip of his cosmic cooler. "What do you think that planet is like?"

"Who knows?" said Zack. "I dream about it though, and in my dreams it's really cool. . . . There are all kinds of dinosaurs there, and the planet

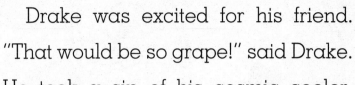

is filled with waterfalls and strange trees."

"Do you know when you would leave?" Drake asked.

"No," said Zack, thinking. "The ultra-shuttle isn't ready yet."

Just then Seth Stevens walked by. He was telling his friends about the baby pterosaur. "Yeah, I saw him up close. He is kind of wimpy. They are taking him home in two weeks."

*Two weeks?* wondered Zack. *How will I be able to wait two weeks?*

After what seemed like the longest day ever, school finally ended. Zack rushed home. He paced back and forth in his room, hoping his hyperphone would ring.

Zack stared at his

hyperphone as if that might force it to ring. Then he paced some more.

*What could be keeping him?* Zack wondered.

Suddenly his hyperphone rang. *This is it!* Zack answered it.

"Hey, Dad," he said nervously.

"Hi, Captain," Dad replied. "So,

what are you doing the day after tomorrow?"

Zack thought for a second. Two days from now was Sunday.

"Do you think you can come with me to the Prehistoric Planet?" Dad asked.

Zack almost jumped out of his skin. "Mr. Stevens said yes?" cried Zack.

"He sure did!" Dad replied.

"But I didn't think the ultra-shuttle would be ready so fast," Zack explained.

"We're putting the finishing touches on it tomorrow. Then the day after it'll blast off to the Prehistoric Planet!

"And *I'm* coming with you!" Zack exclaimed. "YIPPEE WAH-WAH!"

# Chapter 7
# Ready to Fly!

Zack got up early on Sunday. He was so excited—he was ready to go two hours before his dad was even awake! As Luna watched, Zack charged up his camtram. He made sure all the settings were correct. He didn't want to miss this once-in-a-lifetime chance

317

to get pictures of a real live dinosaur on its home planet.

"Dinosaurs lived even before there were dogs," Zack said to Luna.

*Yip! Yip!* barked Luna.

"I wish I could take you with me on this trip," said Zack. "But it's a people-only journey. Except, of course, for the pterosaur we're taking home."

*Urrr—urrr,* Luna

whined, as if she knew she couldn't go.

Zack set the focus on his camtram to the setting that made the images look extra-sharp. Then he put it into his carry bag and waited.

Time passed super-slowly.

Finally, Dad's voice rang out from the commu-link speaker in the wall of Zack's bedroom. "Ready to fly, Captain?"

"You bet!" Zack yelled back.

He dashed into the elevator with Luna right behind him. It traveled sideways through the house and arrived at the garage. Dad was waiting, along with Mom, Cathy, and Charlotte.

"Permission to go to the Prehistoric Planet, Captain?" asked Dad, smiling.

"Permission granted, Mr. Nelson," Zack joked back at his dad.

"Now have a safe trip, you two explorers," said Mom.

"And take . . ."

". . . that baby dinosaur . . ."

". . . home to its mother," added Cathy and Charlotte.

Dad climbed into his red Nebulonics car. He left the door open for Zack.

"Forget something?" Dad asked.

"Oh wow!" exclaimed Zack. "I'm so excited, I almost forgot my camtram. I'll be right back."

Zack ran into the house, picked up his carry bag, and raced back out to the car. He climbed in and closed the door behind him.

"What are you waiting for, Dad?" asked Zack. "We've got a dinosaur to

take home!"

Dad smiled and launched the car into the sky. A few minutes later they arrived at Nebulonics. Zack and his dad entered the huge building and headed to the shuttle bay. There, Zack met the other members of the crew.

"Everyone, this is my son, Zack Nelson," Dad began. "He'll be joining us on the mission. Zack, this is Captain Zorflane. He'll be our pilot."

"Good to have you aboard, Zack," Captain Zorflane said.

"And this is Raxite Yakko, our copilot," Dad continued.

"Hi, Zack. Welcome," said a tall Nebulite. Both men were wearing the

**325**

uniform of the Nebulon Navigators. "I remember you. You are the young man who found that giant gemmite on Juno."

"Yes, sir," Zack said proudly. "I'm a new member of the Sprockets Academy Explorers Club."

*It's hard to believe I'm going on another trip with the Nebulon Navigators!* Zack thought.

# Chapter 8
# A
# Stowaway

Suddenly the hatch to the ultra-shuttle opened.

*WHOOOSH!*

*This is so grape!*

Then a large shuttle-bay door slid open. In rolled a cage on wheels. Inside the cage sat the most amazing

creature Zack had ever seen.

Zack's jaw dropped open. He pointed at the creature.

"Wow!" said Zack. "A real live dinosaur from the past."

"Not from the past, Zack," explained Captain Zorflane. "This pterosaur is right here, right now. And I think it

is now ready to go home."

The pterosaur spread its wings and opened its mouth wide.

*Ka-caaaaw! Ka-caaaaw!*

The dinosaur's cry echoed around the shuttle bay.

Captain Zorlane, I think you're right!" said Zack, smiling.

"Then what are we waiting for?" asked Dad. "Let's go!"

Zack and the rest of the crew climbed on board. Zack strapped himself into his seat. Then the pterosaur's cage was loaded onto the ship. The ultra-shuttle's hatch closed.

"Three . . . two . . . one . . . BLAST OFF!"

The ultra-shuttle's

engines fired. Within a few seconds Zack was in space. He immediately felt right at home.

The ultra-shuttle was almost twenty times as big as the Nelson family's space cruiser. That ship had carried the family from Earth to their new home on Nebulon.

This spacecraft had seats for fifty passengers. It also had a huge cargo area. That's where the pterosaur's cage sat.

*I love space travel!* thought Zack. He looked out the window as they whizzed by stars and planets.

*Ka-caaaaw! Ka-caaaaw!*

The pterosaur's cry filled the ship.

"It's okay," Zack called out. "We're taking you home."

Zack looked over at the cage. The scared pterosaur spread its huge

wings and opened its long beak.

*Ka-caaaaw! Ka-caaaaw!* it cried again.

*Urrr—urrr,* came a whining moan.

"Wait a minute," said Zack. "What's that?"

*Urrr—urrr.*

"That's not the pterosaur. . . . That sounds like Luna!"

Just then Luna crawled out from under Zack's seat.

"What are you doing here, girl?"

*Yip! Yip!* Luna barked.

"How in the world did she end up on board the ultra-shuttle?" Dad asked.

Zack thought for a moment. "Well, the door to the Nebulonics car was open while I ran back into the house to get my camtram," Zack recalled. "And then the hatch to the shuttle was open while we were all looking at the pterosaur in the shuttle bay."

"She must have snuck into the car, then snuck on board the ultra-shuttle!" exclaimed Dad.

"Luna, you sneaky girl. You're coming with us after all!" Zack cried.

"I guess you're not the only one who's excited about seeing dinosaurs," Dad said to Zack. The crew chuckled.

Luna jumped onto Zack's lap. She stared out the window at the stars streaking past.

# Chapter 9
# The Prehistoric Planet

Several hours later the Prehistoric Planet came into view.

"Crew, please prepare for landing," Captain Zorflane announced.

*I'm part of the crew,* thought Zack. *This is so grape!*

The ship dropped through the

343

clouds. Zack watched as the planet came closer and closer. A few seconds later the ultra-shuttle landed.

The hatch opened with a hiss. Zack and the other members of the crew stepped outside.

A thick jungle spread out in every direction. Tall trees swayed gently in the hot, steamy breeze. Their big, broad leaves waved like fans.

Zack pulled the camtram

from his bag and begin recording. "I can't believe it!" cried Zack. "This planet looks exactly like the planet in my dream!"

Suddenly the soft breeze whipped up into a huge gust of wind. The trees began to bend and shake.

"There's some strange weather on this planet," said Zack. "It changes so quickly."

*KA-CAAAAW! KA-CAAAAW!*

A deafening screech shattered the silence.

"It's the pterosaur!" cried Zack. But when he looked around, he didn't see the pterosaur.

"We have not taken the pterosaur out of the ship yet," said one of the Nebulon Navigators.

Then a much softer cry came from inside the ultra-shuttle.

*Ka-caaaaw! Ka-caaaaw!*

It sounded to Zack like the baby pterosaur was trying to answer the louder call.

"We need to get our passenger out of the ship!" shouted Captain Zorflane.

The Nebulon Navigators quickly

rolled the cage out of the shuttle.

Again a blast of wind swept through the jungle. Then came another ear-splitting shriek.

*KA-CAAAAW! KA-CAAAAW!*

The baby pterosaur in the cage spread its wings and let out a long, sad cry.

*Ka-caaaaaaaaaw! Ka-caaaaaaw!*

"Open the cage!" shouted Captain Zorflane.

The Nebulon Navigators opened the latch and threw open the cage door.

The pterosaur flapped its wings and took off into the sky.

*KA-CAAAAW! KA-CAAAAW!* came the loud roar once again.

The baby pterosaur flew off toward the sound of the roar. Luna dashed through the jungle trying to follow

the pterosaur. She crashed through branches and leaves. Zack and the crew followed close behind.

*It's weird that this is so much like my dream,* thought Zack.

When Zack and the others reached a clearing, the wind picked up again.

*KA-CAAAAW! KA-CAAAAW!*

This time
the loud roar was
directly overhead.

Zack looked up and saw a pterosaur flapping its wings in the sky. Only
this one was twice as big as the one
they had brought on the shuttle!

*Ka-caaaaw! Ka-caaaaw!*

The baby pterosaur flew into view. It
screeched happily.

"We did it!" cried Zack. "We brought the baby pterosaur home to its mother!"

The two pterosaurs flew around each other in a circle. Then they flew off over the jungle.

"Let's follow them!" suggested Zack. He pointed his camtram into the air to record the flying dinosaurs.

Zack and the others plunged back into the jungle, following the pterosaurs overhead. As he walked, Zack recorded pictures of trees and plants. Luna walked along beside him sniffing at the ground.

"Hey!" said Zack, stepping up to a plant with many layers. "I recognize this plant. I learned about it in my science

class back on Earth. It's called a horsetail, Luna."

*Yip! Yip!* Luna barked happily in response.

Glancing overhead, Zack saw the two pterosaurs make a sharp turn.

*I wonder where they're going,* he thought.

Zack walked along, looking up so he could keep an eye on the pterosaurs.

Suddenly the ground under his feet changed from soft leaves to hard gravel. When he looked down again he was shocked to see that he was at the edge of a cliff!

Zack immediately stopped, but he lost his footing. He started to slip over the edge of the cliff!

# Chapter 10
# Home—to Nebulon

"YAAAA!" cried Zack as he felt his feet give way.

"Zack!" yelled Dad, dashing toward his son.

Luna latched on to Zack's jacket with her teeth. She held him steady long enough for Dad to reach him.

Dad grabbed Zack and pulled him back to safety.

"Be careful, buddy," Dad said to Zack. "Let's all try to get back to Nebulon in one piece!"

"Thanks, Dad. Thanks, Luna," said Zack, scratching her head.

*Yip! Yip!* Luna barked.

The pterosaurs disappeared into

the distance. Zack gazed across the
valley below the cliff.

"Dad! Look at that!" he cried,
pointing.

Across the valley he saw a huge
waterfall, just like the one from his
dream. Only this one was even bigger.

"Wow!" Dad said. "That's the biggest waterfall I've ever seen— on Earth or on Nebulon."

"And look at all the dinosaurs down at the bottom!" exclaimed Zack.

A family of brachiosaurs drank peacefully from the lake at the bottom of the waterfall. Their long necks bent gracefully toward the water.

Beside them, two baby triceratops splashed around in the lake. They gently nudged each other with the three huge horns on their heads.

Suddenly the ground began to shake.

"Are we having an earthquake?" Dad asked.

"No, look!" said Zack, pointing down to a ridge just below.

There, two big Tyrannosaurus rex wrestled with each other. Their size and power made the ground shake.

"Wow! They're huge!" exclaimed Zack. "I studied the Tyrannosaurus rex back on Earth. The name means 'King of the Thunder Lizard.' They're called 'T. rex' for short."

The ground rumbled beneath their feet.

Luna ran to the edge of the cliff. She looked down and barked at the T. rex.

*Yip! Yip!*

The T. rex looked up. It stared right at Luna.

*GRRRRRRRROOOOAAAARRRR!*

it growled, then roared at Luna.

The frightened dog jumped up

into Zack's arms and began to whimper.

"Oh! It's okay, girl," Zack said, scratching behind her ear. "I think you should stick to barking at squirrels."

"Okay, everyone," Captain Zorflane announced. "We have completed our mission. It is time to go home."

"I can't wait to get back to
Nebulon and tell everyone
all about our adventure,"
Zack told his dad. Then
he suddenly realized
that, for the first time
since he moved from
Earth, Zack thought of
Nebulon as his home.

Back on the ultra-shuttle
Zack settled into his seat.
Luna curled up on his lap.

"Three . . . two . . . one . . . BLAST
OFF!"

Soon Zack and the rest of the crew were zooming through space. They were on their way back home—to Nebulon.

Zack gazed out the window. "That was some adventure, huh, Luna?" he said.

Suddenly Zack's hyperphone began to buzz. He pulled it out

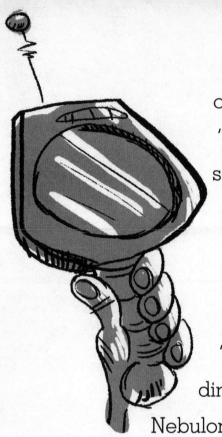

of his carry bag.

"It's Bert," Zack said. "He's calling from Earth."

"Hey, Zack," said Bert over the hyperphone. "I heard that a dinosaur landed on Nebulon. It was all over the news here on Earth. Did you get to see it?"

"Not only did I get to see it," began Zack, "but I was part of the team that brought it back to its home planet—a

planet where dinosaurs still live! I'm
on the ultra-shuttle that my dad helped
design! It's soooooo grape!"

"Okay, first," said Bert, "I'm still
going to have to get used to that
saying. And second . . . how COOL is
that? I wish I was there!"

"Don't worry," said Zack. "I have it

all in my
camtram. I'll
z-mail you the videos
as soon as I get home."

Nebulon really is
starting to feel like
home, Zack thought.
Now THAT'S pretty grape!

# GALAXY ZACK

## MONSTERS IN SPACE!

# CONTENTS

# Chapter 1
# Class Monster!

Zack Nelson raced through the front door of Sprockets Academy. He was late for school.

Zack had dozed off that morning after his alarm went off. Breakfast took longer than usual, and his dog, Luna, had insisted on a last-minute walk.

Zack dashed across the wide lobby and ran into a round opening in the wall. A door hissed shut and he took off. The clear round elevator looked more like a giant plastic ball. It sped through a tube going sideways. Then a few seconds later it stopped.

A door whooshed open, and Zack burst into his classroom. Everyone in the class was already in his or her usual seat. Zack ran toward his seat and suddenly stopped in his tracks.

*There's someone in my seat!* Zack thought. He looked closely. *No! Not someone, some-THING! A monster!*

A huge purple monster sat in his seat. The monster was at least four times as big as Zack. It was furry with green patches, and it had five eyes. Its floppy ears stuck out from its face.

*I've got to save my class before the monster does something terrible,* Zack thought. *But how?*

Zack spotted Drake Taylor. Ever since Zack and his family moved from

Earth to Nebulon, Drake had been his best new friend. Zack hurried to Drake's side.

"Drake! What is that thing doing here?" Zack whispered, pointing at the monster.

The monster yawned. Its mouth was filled with big, sharp teeth.

"What's it going to do to us?" Zack asked.

Drake gave Zack a puzzled look. Before Drake could reply, their teacher, Ms. Rudolph, came into the room.

"Okay, class, let's begin," she said. "Please turn on your edu-screens. Today we are going to continue our study of the second age of Nebulon history."

Zack stared at Ms. Rudolph in disbelief.

*Doesn't she see it?* he wondered. *Isn't she afraid of the monster?*

Ms. Rudolph soon began her lesson.

Zack looked around at his classmates. They were all paying attention. No one seemed bothered by the fact that a big purple monster was right there in the room.

Zack slipped into an empty seat.

Ms. Rudolph continued the lesson.

*What's wrong with everyone? Zack wondered. Why aren't they scared?*

387

# Chapter 2
# Lunch Monster!

The class continued as if everything were normal. Ms. Rudolph and Zack's classmates went through the lesson like they did each day.

*You would think that it was normal for there to be a monster in our class!* Zack thought. He tried his best to

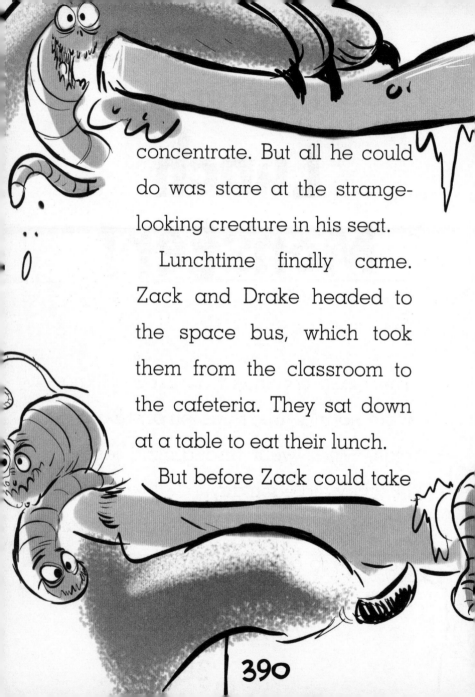

concentrate. But all he could do was stare at the strange-looking creature in his seat.

Lunchtime finally came. Zack and Drake headed to the space bus, which took them from the classroom to the cafeteria. They sat down at a table to eat their lunch.

But before Zack could take

a bite of his nebu-nut-butter sandwich, he spotted the monster. It was sitting just two tables away!

The monster pulled out a sandwich. Yellow worms squiggled between the pieces of blue bread. The monster took a big bite of the worm sandwich.

*Yuck!* Zack thought. *That is so disgusting!*

"So what were you trying to tell me before?" asked Drake.

Zack grabbed Drake's arm and pointed to the big purple creature at the nearby table.

"There was a monster in our

classroom!" Zack whispered. "And nobody seemed to notice. Now it's right here in the cafeteria. And still nobody cares. No one is scared. Except me!"

Drake laughed. "That is not a monster, Zack," Drake explained. "In case you never noticed, there are lots of different kinds of people on Nebulon.

That kid is a Plexi. He is from the planet Plexus. It is not too far from Nebulon."

"What's he doing here?" Zack asked. He was still uneasy having that scary-looking thing right there in his school.

"Oh, right," Drake said. "You came in late so you missed it. He told us that he is visiting Nebulon. He will be sitting in our class for a few days."

Zack took a bite of his sandwich. He continued to stare at the Plexi.

"I've never seen a monster before," said Zack. "At least, not a real one. It's like my nightmares are coming true!"

"Hold on," said Drake. "He is not a monster. He is just a guy who looks different from you. After all, you and I do not look the same, right?"

Zack thought about this for a moment. He realized that Drake was right. Drake was a Nebulite. His head was more egg-shaped that Zack's. His arms were longer and hung down to his knees.

When Zack first met Drake, he noticed these differences. But once they became friends, Zack never even thought about them.

"Yeah, Drake, but you're not huge and purple and furry," Zack said, "and you don't have five eyes."

"What is the difference, Zack?" Drake asked.

Zack leaned in close to his friend. "Uhh . . . you are not a monster," Zack whispered.

He looked over at the monster. The big purple creature took another bite from his slimy, squiggly, worm sandwich.

"Yuck!" said Zack.

# Chapter 3
# Monster . . . or Not?

Zack hurried home after school. He ran inside his house. Luna was waiting in the kitchen. She stood up on her back legs and licked Zack's face.

"Hi, girl. I missed you too!" Zack said, scratching Luna's head.

"Welcome home, Master Just Zack,"

said Ira. Ira was the Nelson family's Indoor Robotic Assistant. "Would you like a spudsy melonade?"

"Sure!" cried Zack.

A panel in the wall slid open. A robot arm popped out holding a glass of lime-colored, frosty, bubbling juice.

Zack took the glass and gulped down the juice. "Thanks, Ira. Spudsy melonade is grape!"

On Nebulon, kids said "grape" when they thought that something was really cool. Zack had lived on Nebulon for only a few months. But the planet was really starting to feel like home.

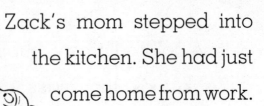

Zack's mom stepped into the kitchen. She had just come home from work. Mrs. Nelson owned a boutique that sold Earth clothing to the women of Nebulon.

"Hi, honey. How was school today?" she asked.

Zack was so excited to get home and see Luna that he had forgotten all about the monster in his class.

Until now.

"There was a monster in my class!" he said.

"Really?" replied his mom.

Zack could tell from her voice that she didn't believe him.

"Maybe you shouldn't be reading so many 3-D holo-comics," said Mom.

Zack loved reading the comics on Nebulon. Each page came to life. Superheroes, dinosaurs, monsters, and more battled it out in 3-D, right before his eyes.

"No, Mom, I'm being serious," said Zack. "He was big and purple. And he was furry and covered with green patches. He had five eyes and floppy ears."

"And what makes you think he's a monster, Zack?" asked Mom.

"I just told you," Zack said. He couldn't understand how his mom was missing the point. "He's big and purple and has five—"

"All that means is that he looks different from you," explained Mom. "Just because he's different doesn't mean he's a monster. Drake doesn't look like you. Is he a monster?"

"No, of course not, but—"

"There are lots of different kinds of people on Nebulon," continued Mom, "just

409

410

like there are lots of different kinds of people back on Earth. That doesn't make any of them monsters, does it?"

"Well, no. I guess not," said Zack. He scratched his head, feeling a bit confused.

"We can talk more about this later, if you'd like," suggested Mom. "Luna has been waiting for you all day. Why don't you two play outside?"

Zack ran out the door.

"Come on, Luna!" he called.

Luna raced after him.

Zack held up a small ball. It flashed orange, then blue, then red, then green.

"Ready, girl?" asked Zack. The flashing ball was Luna's favorite toy.

*Yip! Yip!* barked Luna.

"Go get it!" Zack tossed the ball across the yard. Luna took off after it.

As the ball spun through the air, its many colors blended together.

Zack thought hard about what his mom had said.

413

# Chapter 4
# A Zandy Friend

The next day, Zack was on time for school. He walked into the classroom with his schoolmates. There, sitting in his seat again, was the monster.

"Okay, everyone take your seats," Ms. Rudolph announced. "Boys and girls, once again we have a guest in our classroom." Then she pointed right at the monster.

The monster stood slowly. He was even bigger than Zack had remembered. He walked to the front of the class and stood next to the teacher. The monster was twice as tall as Ms. Rudolph!

"I'm sure you may remember him from yesterday," said Ms. Rudolph.

*Remember?* thought Zack. *I haven't been able to think about anything else!*

"Today I want you to pay attention while he tells us a little bit about himself," Ms. Rudolph said.

The monster looked around the class. Then he smiled, showing off his big, sharp teeth.

"Hi, everyone," said the monster. "My name is Al."

*Al?* thought Zack. *That's a pretty friendly name for a monster.*

"My dad is here on Nebulon for a business trip. It's only for a week, but I came along because I really like this planet," explained Al.

Zack was amazed. Al's voice was soft and gentle. It wasn't the loud,

deep, scary voice Zack remembered
from monster movies he saw on Earth.
In fact, Zack realized that Al sounded
a lot like . . . well, a lot like him!

Zack thought again about what his
mom had said. He remembered how
worried he was when he first moved
to Nebulon. Zack had thought the kids
wouldn't like him because he was

421

different from them. He recalled how happy he was that Drake sat next to him on the bus and wanted to be his friend.

Al took his seat again and Ms. Rudolph began the day's lessons.

When the bell rang for lunch, Zack and Drake hurried to the space bus. Zack saw that Al was sitting by himself.

Zack and Drake sat in the seat across from Al.

"Hey, Al! I'm Zack, and this is my friend Drake," Zack said. "Do you want to eat lunch with us today?"

Al's five eyes opened wide. He smiled. This time, Zack didn't even notice Al's teeth.

"Sure!" said Al.

"So what kind of business trip is your dad on?" asked Zack. Now that he realized that Al really wasn't a monster, he wanted to know more about him.

"He's a salesman," Al explained,
"and I get to travel with him all over
the universe. We're here because he
wants to sell something at that place
called—uh, what's it called?"

Al scratched his furry purple head
as he thought. His ears spun around.

"Nebulonics! That's it," Al said. "A company called Nebulonics."

"My dad works at Nebulonics!" Zack cried.

*I actually have something in common with Al! Zack thought. Who would have thought?*

Zack smiled. "So I bet you've been to all the planets?" he asked excitedly.

"Well, not all of them," Al said. "There are so many planets to see! But we've been to quite a few. Good thing I love to travel in space."

"Me too!" exclaimed Zack. "My

favorite thing to do is planet hop!"

*So we have a lot in common!* Zack thought. *Just like we were friends.*

"My dad and I are going home this weekend to Plexus," said Al. "Would you and Drake like to come with us?"

"We sure would!" Drake and Zack shouted together.

"But we'll need to ask our parents first," said Zack. "We'll talk to them when we get home."

"Zandy!" said Al.

"'Zandy'?" asked Zack.

"What is 'zandy'?" Drake asked.

"That's what we say on Plexus when we think something is really, really great," explained Al.

"Grape!" said Zack.

"Cool!" added Drake.

# Chapter 5
# Plexus, Here We Come!

After school, Zack raced home. He dashed into his house.

"Mom!" he called out. "Mom, where are you?"

"Your mother is in the gym, Master Just Zack," explained Ira.

"Thanks, Ira," said Zack.

431

Zack hurried to the exercise room.
He found his mother working out.

"Hi, Zack," said Mom. "Is everything
okay?"

"Mom, remember that monster I
told you about at school?" Zack asked.

"Well, honey, I told you that—"

"He's not really a monster," Zack

interrupted. "He's my new friend."

"That's wonderful, Zack," Mom said. "I'm very proud of you."

"His name is Al, and he asked me to visit his home planet for the weekend. His family will be there. And Al also asked Drake. Can I go? Please? Drake is asking his parents too."

"Dad and I can set up a video chat with Al's parents and Drake's parents," suggested Mom. "We can all meet— kind of—and make the arrangements."

"That is so grape, Mom!" cried Zack. "Al's dad is here working with Nebulonics. Maybe Dad already knows him."

Following dinner that evening, Zack's mom and dad settled down in front of the eight-foot-wide sonic cell

monitor in their family room. A box
popped up on the screen. The faces of
Mr. and Mrs. Taylor, Drake's parents,
appeared inside.

Zack peeked around the corner from the next room and watched silently.

"Nice to see you again," Mom said. "I'm so glad Zack and Drake have become such good friends. Drake has really helped him feel more at home here on Nebulon."

"And Drake thinks that Zack is . . ." Mrs. Taylor turned to her husband. "What is that word the kids like to use?"

"Grape," replied Mr. Taylor.

"Yes, grape," Mrs. Taylor said. "Drake thinks Zack is grape."

Zack covered his mouth so his parents wouldn't hear him giggle. Just hearing a grown-up use the word "grape" made him laugh.

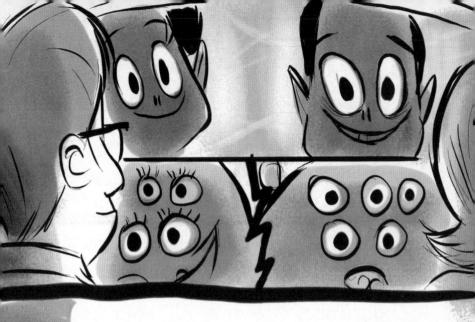

At that moment two more boxes popped up on the big screen. Each box was filled with a big purple face. Each face had five eyes and two floppy ears and were covered in long, fluffy purple fur.

"I am Gur, father of Al," said one face.

"I am Toka, mother of Al," said the other face.

The other four parents introduced themselves too.

Through the monitor, Toka looked right at Zack's mom. She suddenly jumped back slightly.

"Are you all right, Toka?" Mom asked.

"My apologies," Toka said to Mom. "I was startled by how you look. You are . . . so . . . so different from those of us on Plexus."

Zack was amazed. *My mom looks so normal*, he thought.

"Hi, Gur. It's Otto Nelson," Dad said. "We met at Nebulonics today."

"Yes, we did," said Gur. "Our son, Al, would like to invite Zack and Drake to Plexus this weekend. We are so happy Al has made new friends so quickly."

"Yes," added Toka. "We travel to many planets. This may sound strange, but on some planets people are afraid of us. They think we look like . . . like monsters."

"We have met nice people from many worlds who live here on Nebulon," Mom explained, "and we would be happy to have Zack visit you on Plexus."

"We feel the same way about Drake," said Mrs. Taylor.

*YES!!!* thought Zack. *I'm going to Plexus!*

# Chapter 6
# Travel Time!

For the rest of the week all Zack could think about was his trip to Plexus. On Friday he made a list of the things he wanted to bring. He didn't want to forget anything important.

*Let's see,* he thought while sitting in math class. *Camtram, hyperphone,*

*snacks for the ride, pictures of Nebulon and Earth to show Al and his parents.*

Later that night as he drifted off to sleep, Zack imagined all the things he would see on Plexus.

The next morning, Zack, his parents, and his twin sisters, Charlotte and Cathy, went to the Creston City Spaceport. There, they met up with Drake and his parents, and Al and his dad.

"Is everyone ready for a fun weekend?" asked Gur.

"You bet, mister . . . uh . . . uh . . . ," Zack replied. "I'm sorry, I don't know Al's last name."

"We Plexi have only one name," Gur explained. "Please call me Gur."

"I have never been to Plexus," said Drake. "I cannot wait to see it."

"Then let's go!" said Gur.

The three boys walked up the steps to the space cruiser.

"Have a . . ."

". . . fun trip . . ."

". . . and take lots of . . ."

". . . pictures," said Charlotte and Cathy.

"Be careful!" Zack's mom said.

"And send me a z-mail when you get there," added Drake's mom.

Zack and the others stepped on board the space cruiser. A few minutes later, they were on their way to Plexus!

# Chapter 7
# A Whole New World

The space cruiser sped through the galaxy. Zack settled back in his seat and stared out the window. Planets, stars, and swirling colorful clouds of space gas zipped past.

"I can't wait to show you all the zandy stuff we have on Plexus," Al

said. "I'm happy we became friends
so fast. You'll probably laugh at this,
but I've been to some planets where
they thought I was a monster! How
silly is that?"

Zack thought about when he had
first met Al. Then he laughed. "Yeah,"
he said. "Pretty silly."

A short time later the space cruiser began dropping down toward Plexus.

"Hang on, everybody," said Gur. "We'll be landing in a minute."

The first thing Zack noticed as they lowered down through the atmosphere was that Plexus had a yellow sky.

"That's amazing!" said Zack. "I've never seen a yellow sky before!"

The space cruiser gently touched down. Zack grabbed his bag and followed Al and Gur into the spaceport.

Both Zack and Drake stared with their mouths wide open.

People of every size, shape, and
color filled the spaceport. Some were
huge and covered with thick fur.
Others walked on eight legs and made
squeaking noises when they spoke.
Some had three eyes that hung from
their faces on long stalks.

As Zack stared at the people on Plexus, many of them stared back at him. A few pointed and whispered to the person next to them.

Zack thought about how Al's mom had reacted when she first saw his mom. *I have to remember that I look as different to them as they do to me.*

"Come on, guys!" Al said laughing after a couple of minutes. "Don't just stand there staring. I have a lot to show you!"

Zack and Drake followed Al and Gur to their car. It looked more like a sleek space capsule. Everyone climbed in, and the car took off at super-high blinding speed.

"Wow!" said Zack. "Mr. Gur, you drive much faster on your

planet than we do on ours."

"Ha-ha—'Mr. Gur' sounds so unusual. Again, it's okay to just call me Gur. Don't worry; all cars on Plexus are controlled by computer-guided traffi-beams. They keep cars from crashing into one another—even at high speeds."

"Very zandy," said Zack.

A few minutes later they stopped in front of a box

that sat in a row of many other 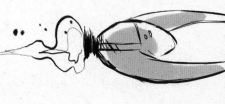 boxes. Each looked big enough to fit four or five people.

"Why are we stopping here?" Drake asked. "I thought we were going to your house."

"This *is* my house," said Al.

*It's awfully small*, thought Zack.

Al laughed. "Come on. I'll show you."

461

# Chapter 8
# Home, Sweet . . . Cave?

Zack, Drake, Al, and Gur all squeezed into the box. It began dropping down into the ground.

"It's an elevator!" said Zack.

"Yup," said Al. "My house is underground!"

The elevator stopped. Its door

whooshed open. Zack and the others

stepped into what looked like a huge

cave. The walls and ceiling were solid

rock. But this was no ordinary cave.

The entire house was filled with

high-tech gadgets. Zack recognized

most of them.

A robotic arm chopped and mixed
food in the kitchen.

"I know that meal-o-matic," said
Zack. "That was made at Nebulonics!"

"Most of this house has Nebulonics
gadgets," explained Gur. "I have
worked with them for many years."

"Welcome home, Gur. Welcome home, Al," said a voice that was very familiar to Zack.

"Ira?" Zack asked.

"Welcome, Zack Nelson. Welcome, Drake Taylor," said Ira.

"Yes," said Gur. "Our house came with an Indoor Robotic Assistant. That was invented at Nebulonics too."

Drake looked around. "You have the coolest house, Al," he said. "It is like living in a high-tech cave!"

"You haven't even seen my room yet!" exclaimed Al.

Al's mom walked into the room and gave Al a hug.

"Hi, Zack. Hi, Drake. I'm so glad you could visit," she said.

Zack and Drake both said hello to Toka.

"We're going to see my room," Al said.

Zack, Drake, and Al hurried down a stone hallway. They walked through a door at the end of the hall and into Al's room.

Zack spotted a computer screen that took up the entire wall.

"Pretty zandy, huh?" said Al. "I can watch movies, video chat with my friends from other planets, and look stuff up for school, all on this wall."

"Grape bed," Drake said, pointing

to a corner of the room. There, a bed hovered in midair.

"An antigravity beam holds it up," Al explained. "It lowers for me to get in and out. Then it floats while I sleep."

"Cool!" cried Zack.

Just then a window showing Al's mom appeared on the giant wall screen.

"Boys, it's time for lunch," she said.

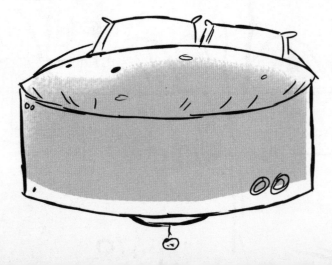

# Chapter 9
# Yummy Worms

Everyone piled back into the car. Soon they were on their way to a diner called Slime Time.

*I wonder what the food will be like,* Zack worried. *I remember that gross worm sandwich Al brought for lunch.*

Once they were seated in the diner,

a waiter with five arms walked past them. He carried a plate in each arm.

*Cool,* thought Zack. *I guess having that many arms would come in handy if you're a waiter.*

The waiter dropped off the food, then came over to their table. He handed everyone a menu.

Zack was nervous. Nothing he saw on the menu was the least bit familiar. The pictures all showed slimy, slithering food.

*Does everyone on this planet eat worms?* he wondered.

Then Al spoke up.

"Can we have three orders of twisty noods, please?" he asked.

"Twisty noods?" asked Drake. He was also worried about what to order. "What is that?"

"Oh, you'll see! They're delicious. I eat them in a sandwich at school sometimes," replied Al.

*Oh no,* Zack thought to himself in a panic. *They really ARE worms! What am I going to do? I can't eat WORMS!*

The waiter brought three plates and set them in front of the boys.

"These are twisty noods?" asked Zack. They looked like spaghetti.

"Mmm . . . ," said Al as he shoved a forkful into his mouth. "These are my favorite! Go ahead, try some!"

*They smell pretty good*, thought Zack. *And I AM pretty hungry.*

He took a bite. "Wow—these are delicious! They taste like chocolate-covered noodles!" said Zack.

"That's because they *are* chocolate-covered noodles!" exclaimed Al.

*Not so strange after all*, thought Zack. He gobbled down the rest of his twisty noods.

After lunch everyone went for a

short walk. They passed a park where a bunch of kids were playing a game. The kids were hitting a soft furry ball back and forth over an electronic net.

Al spotted a couple of his friends in the crowd.

"Hey, guys, these are my new

friends, Zack and Drake!" Al called out.

A short kid with arms that looked like snakes and one large eye in the middle of his stomach turned toward Al and his new friends.

"Monsters!" he cried, pointing at Zack and Drake.

"They're not monsters," replied Al. "They're zandy guys."

"But they look so . . . so . . . different!" said Al's friend.

"Nice to meet you," said Zack.

"Yeah, nice to meet you too," said Al's friend. "Sorry about calling you a monster. I just never saw anyone who looked like you."

"Same here," said Zack, smiling.

483

That evening Al's parents took the three boys to a movie called *Worm Blast!*

As the movie began, a robot arm popped from the seat and handed Zack a snack.

"What's this?" Zack whispered to Al.

"It's brick bark," Al whispered back. "It's chocolate and plexu-nuts."

"Thanks," said Zack. He missed

popcorn but enjoyed the tasty treat.

Up on the screen, a giant worm exploded from the ground. Zack felt his seat shake. It felt like the action on the screen was really happening to him!

*This so grape!* he thought. *Going to the movies on Plexus is . . .* zandy!

Back at Al's house, the boys looked at the pictures and videos Zack had taken that day with his camtram.

"I can't wait to show this to Bert," said Zack.

"Who's Bert?" asked Al.

"Bert is my friend from Earth," Zack explained. "That's where I was born."

Soon the boys grew sleepy. They were exhausted from their day.

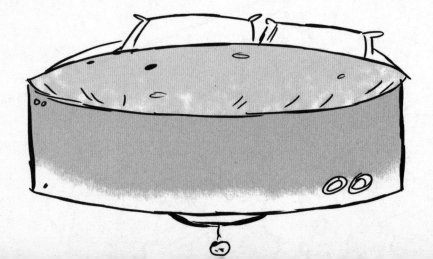

# Chapter 10
# Good-Bye, Friend

The next morning Zack, Drake, Al, and Gur piled into the space shooter and headed back to Nebulon. Zack arrived home and told his family all about his adventures on Plexus.

"Sounds like . . ."

". . . you made . . ."

". . . a good new friend," said Charlotte and Cathy.

"I sure did," said Zack. "And I learned some things too. It doesn't matter what someone *looks* like. What matters is who they are inside."

Zack's mom gave him a great big hug.

After school the next day Al came to Zack's house. As soon as he spotted Luna, he hid behind a counter.

"What's that?" asked Al, pointing at Luna.

"Don't be scared," said Zack. "Luna's my dog. She's very friendly. Pet her. . . . You'll see."

Al approached Luna slowly.

"I've never seen anything like her," he explained.

Al bent down and petted Luna gently on her head. She wagged her tail happily.

"See? She likes you!" said Zack.

Al smiled. Then he remembered why he had come over.

"My dad and I have to go home tomorrow,"

Al said, "but I hope we'll be back soon. . . ."

Zack started to feel sad. He remembered how he felt when he had to leave Earth . . . when he had to say goodbye to Bert.

"I had a really great time here on Nebulon," said Al.

"And I had a fun time on Plexus," replied Zack. "Let's video chat soon."

"Sounds zandy," said Al. "Bye."

Once Al had left, Zack headed to his room. He flopped onto his bed. He was

still feeling sad when the viewscreen
in his bedroom began to blink.

"You have an incoming vid-mez,
Master Just Zack," Ira announced.

Zack bounced from his bed and
touched the screen. A box opened
showing a picture of Bert and a
message.

Zack listened to Bert's voice: "Hi, Zack. Guess what! I'm coming to visit you on Nebulon!"

"No WAAAAAY!" cried Zack. He couldn't be more excited.

*I can't wait to show him all the zandy . . . I mean grape . . . I mean cool stuff on Nebulon!*

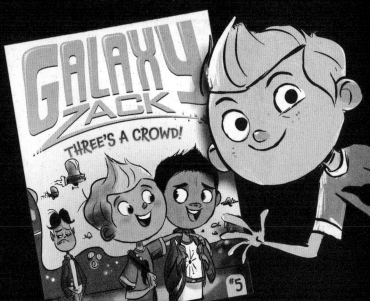

# Waiting for Bert

Zack Nelson jumped up from his seat at the kitchen table. He had hardly taken a bite from the stack of nebu-cakes that sat on his plate.

"I can't believe he's coming today!" Zack cried. He threw both his arms into the air. Then he spun around in a circle

An excerpt from *Three's a Crowd!*

and shouted, "YIPPEE WAH-WAH!"

"Honey, I know you're excited that Bert is coming to visit," said Shelly Nelson, Zack's mom. "But you haven't touched any of your breakfast. Nebu-cakes with boingoberry syrup are your favorite. And it's almost time to leave for school."

"But *Bert* is coming!" Zack shouted. "I haven't seen him in so long!"

Bert Jones was Zack's best friend on Earth. But Zack didn't live on Earth anymore. A few months ago Zack and his family had moved to the planet Nebulon. Zack had not seen Bert since he moved.

An excerpt from *Three's a Crowd!*

At least not in person.

Sure they kept in touch through z-mail and video chats. Zack even had a holocam that showed a 3-D image of Bert. It almost felt like Bert was in the room.

But not really.

Zack missed going to baseball games with Bert. He missed trading 3-D holo-comics. He missed going to the orbiting drive-in movie

theater for triple features. He just
missed having his best buddy nearby,
even if they had nothing to do.

Zack missed Bert. And now Bert
was coming from Earth to visit him on
Nebulon. Zack couldn't wait to show
Bert around his new home planet.

An excerpt from *Three's a Crowd!*

"Come on, honey. You have to eat something!" Mom insisted.

Zack leaned over his plate. He grabbed an entire nebu-cake and shoved it into his mouth. A thin line of purple boingoberry syrup ran down his chin.

"Dmvrum barimden," he mumbled through a mouthful of food.

"Don't talk with your mouth full," said Mom.

Zack swallowed.

"Okay," he said. "Gotta go. Can't be late for school. The Sprockets Speedybus will be here any second. Bye, Mom!"

An excerpt from *Three's a Crowd!*

"Have a good day at school," Mom said.

Zack grabbed his jacket and his backpack and dashed out the front door. His twin sisters, Charlotte and Cathy, followed him outside.

"Bye, Mom. . . ."

"We'll see you . . ."

An excerpt from *Three's a Crowd!*

".  .  . after school," said Charlotte and Cathy.

The school speedybus was waiting outside.

*Now all I have to do is make it through the school day!* Zack thought. Then he and his sisters climbed on board the bus.

An excerpt from *Three's a Crowd!*

HERE ARE SOME MORE OUT-OF-THIS-WORLD

# GALAXY ZACK

## ADVENTURES!

GALAXY ZACK
THREE'S A CROWD!

GALAXY ZACK
A GREEN CHRISTMAS!

GALAXY ZACK
A GALACTIC EASTER!

GALAXY ZACK
DRAKE MAKES A SPLASH!

GALAXY ZACK
THE ANNOYING CRUSH!

GALAXY ZACK
A HAUNTED HALLOWEEN

GALAXY ZACK
RETURN TO EARTH!

GALAXY ZACK
OPERATION TWIN TROUBLE

# GALAXY ZACK

## READING IS OUT OF THIS WORLD!